HUNGRY
CONSTELLATIONS

Mike Allen

Introduction by Amal El-Mohtar

Selections by Dominik Parisien

Mythic Delirium Books
mythicdelirium.com

Hungry Constellations

Cover © 2014 by Paula Arwen Friedlander
arwendesigns.net

Title page illustration: "The Dragon's Head and Tail" from *Liber Astronomiae* by Guido Bonatti, 1550

ISBN-10: 0988912422
ISBN-13: 978-0-9889124-2-7

Published by Mythic Delirium Books
mythicdelirium.com

in collaboration with Antimatter Press
antimatterpress.com

Our gratitude goes out to the following who because of their generosity are from now on designated as supporters of Mythic Delirium Books: Saira Ali, Cora Anderson, Anonymous, Patricia M. Cryan, Steve Dempsey, Oz Drummond, Patrick Dugan, Matthew Farrer, C. R. Fowler, Mary J. Lewis, Paul T. Muse, Jr., Shyam Nunley, Finny Pendragon, Kenneth Schneyer, and Delia Sherman.

Praise for Mike Allen

Allen's is poetry for goths of all ages . . . There is a long tradition of poetry dealing with the uncanny—think Keats' "La Belle Dame Sans Merci" or Coleridge's "The Rime of the Ancient Mariner"—and it's nice to see someone putting it to such use again. Allen's poems . . . do a fine job of making the human scary and the scary human.

— *The Philadelphia Inquirer*

Mike Allen pours everything he's got onto his poem-canvases. Mythologies, science-fiction scenarios, private memories and desires, and untestable ideas crowd and overlay one another upon the pages as if flung from an overloaded brush. Here is a vividly vertiginous collection of poems, all fun and mind-games.

—Fred Chappell

Mike Allen is a poetic Shiva, whirling his thousand limbs to snatch gold from thin air and create these epics-in-miniature, each with its own metallic sheen.

—Catherynne M. Valente

In the great tradition of Clark Ashton Smith, Ray Bradbury and Ursula K. Le Guin, Mike Allen shows us how science fiction poetry can do what all first-rate poetry does—rouse the imagination to venture into darkness and the unknown, there to discover old truths and new delights.

—R.H.W. Dillard

Mike Allen's poetry is sometimes amusing, often disturbing, but never disappointing. Certain passages get under your skin and call you back to read them again and again, each time to find new insights, hidden meanings whispered in allegorical phrase.

—*Strange Horizons*

The literary equivalent of a Caravaggio painting, where light is bright and casts all the more shadow for its brilliance . . . These are the horrors of Allen's universe, the looming darkness of unknowing and the impending sense that all human effort to know will, as with Sisyphus' labors, never be enough.

—*The Pedestal Magazine*

Also by Mike Allen

Novels

THE BLACK FIRE CONCERTO
THE GHOULMAKER'S ARIA (forthcoming)

Short Fiction Collections

UNSEAMING

Poetry Collections

THE JOURNEY TO KAILASH
STRANGE WISDOMS OF THE DEAD
DISTURBING MUSES
PETTING THE TIME SHARK
DEFACING THE MOON

As Editor

MYTHIC DELIRIUM (with Anita Allen)

CLOCKWORK PHOENIX 4

CLOCKWORK PHOENIX 3:
New Tales of Beauty and Strangeness

CLOCKWORK PHOENIX 2:
More Tales of Beauty and Strangeness

CLOCKWORK PHOENIX:
Tales of Beauty and Strangeness

MYTHIC 2

MYTHIC

THE ALCHEMY OF STARS:
Rhysling Award Winners Showcase (with Roger Dutcher)

NEW DOMINIONS:
Fantasy Stories by Virginia Writers

CONTENTS

New and Uncollected Poems

Introduction

Amal El-Mohtar

At the time of this writing, Mike and I have been friends—and each other's editors—for eight years. During that time we've had several conversations about how to introduce collections of other people's work: Mike—as demonstrated through the first three *Clockwork Phoenix* anthologies—favours a ringmaster style, introduction via performance and immersion, while I, staid and boring, tend to prefer thoughtful analysis and musings on process. I find myself thinking of those conversations now, as I attempt to do justice to a compilation of poems that spans the same length of time as our friendship—especially because, in many ways, introducing Mike Allen is as superfluous an enterprise as introducing that ringmaster to the audience of his circus.

Perhaps what is required here is not so much an introduction as a warning; not so much an opening act as a shadowy figure lurking by the entrance to the Big Top, beckoning you over for a word before you go in.

Let me tell you about Mike Allen's poetry. This is a man who delights in breaking bodies: butchering, splitting, flaying, dismembering, then seeding landscapes with viscera until they too become bodies—bodies invaded, bodies stuffed, bodies contaminated. This is a man who carves words into and out of bodies, be they skin or sapphire, corpses or constellations. But somehow Allen skirts gore and clinical detachment both: there is a precision and an economy to his horror that's reminiscent of clockwork, architecture, astronomy. Imagine a clock with bone-gears, a skin-tree growing liver-fruit, a ship knifing a face into the moon, and you'll have something of a sense of what lies before you.

This book, for all that it's ephemeral, is also a body—lying innocently in your hands while penetrating you, inhabiting you, and taking you for a ride.

This is a collection in three acts: the first two are potent distillations of previous collections, while the third is a collection in its own right, consisting of Allen's most recent and—in my view—ambitious work. They're all gorgeously, alchemically curated by

Dominik Parisien, in so deep and layered a way that I would almost count him more collaborator than editor. Every section has its own internal logic and movement, and each stands on its own as a piece of a story one could tell about Mike Allen's poetry—a myth of origin, a myth of development, a myth of transcendence. But this is no Hero's Journey; you're not among heroes here. Subterranean in conception and galactic in execution, this is a book of monsters.

So step inside the tent; the ringmaster will be along shortly. It won't be what you expect, but don't use up all your alarm at once.

You'll begin among the dead; you'll take a long walk off a short pier; you'll land among the stars.

You'd do well to have forgotten how to breathe by then.

Selections from *Strange Wisdoms of the Dead*

The Strip Search

The Gate said "Abandon All Hope."

I thought I'd tossed all my hope away,
but when I stepped through the Gate, it still pinged.
One of the guards slithered out of its seat,
snarling as it drew forth a wand.
C'mere, it hissed,
it seems you're still holding out hope.

Its crusted hide was a Venus landscape up close.
It brushed that cold black wand all over my skin,
put it in places I don't want to talk about.
Snaggle fangs huffed in my face:
Sir, step over here, please.

Then the strip search began.
My flesh rolled up & tossed aside for mushy sifting.
Bones X-rayed, stacked in narrow rows, marrow
sucked out, tested, spit back in.
They made me open mind, heart, soul, shook them out
like sacks of flour, panned the contents
for every nugget of twinkling hope, glistening courage;
applying lethal aerosol
to any motion that could be ascribed to love or will
or malingering dreams—
sparing only a few squirming morsels
for later snacking.

Once they were done
they made me pick up my own pieces
(I did the best I could without a mirror)
then my guard kicked me out—
with a literal kick—
sent me rolling down the path to my final destination.

I'll be honest with you, it's no picnic here.
But, my friends, I still have hope. I do.

I'm not going to tell you
where I hid it.

The Strange Wisdom of the Dead

A cruel joke
returned his soul (briefly)
to his body,
and he clawed words
in his coffin lid:
THE EYES OF GOD
ARE FANGED MOUTHS

finale

"It will be the supreme thrill, the only one I haven't tried."
—Serial killer Albert Fish, awaiting his death by electrocution,
1936.

Today is a day to sample death,
stick your flimsy fingers in the box
to draw out one sweet after another,
nip at the flavors of blood and burning,
lap up the juice that stains your palms.

Today is a day to swallow death,
let the bone catch in your throat,
let the bleach gnaw you from inside,
fill yourself with nails and needles
until quicksilver brims in your eyes.

Today is a day to suckle death,
gnash soft teeth on that leathery teat,
the milk to wash down your treats
sour as multitudes in unmarked graves,
bitter as bodies in the tide.

Peel away the husk of grief,
that shriek of self gouged away,
clutching at the raw, useless edge;
and what remains is slicker, smoother
than the silkiest of skin; something

you can't keep your hands from,
something you crave to cover
your every inch, as welcome
a lover as the earth that parts
the cracks in the coffin.

Death of the Father

Your naked, blackened ribs
    arch overhead,
architecture
    of the grandest decay.
I stand here,
    where your heart once pulsed
and admire the symmetry
    of your remains,
the regal thrust
    of your smoldering jaw,
the once-fertile majesty
    of your flame-scoured pelvis,
the dark mysteries
    glimpsed through the fissures
of your shattered skull.
    I walk across
the former belly
    of a former god,
my footsteps hissing in the mud
    of your combusted flesh,
and marvel
    how the mountains must have shook
with your death throes,
    how the columns of your temples
must have toppled,
    cities of marble and granite
capsizing,
    fissures swallowing
the geometric groves,
    all your worshipers
following you to the last,
    into oblivion.
I, the seed of fire
    my mother planted in you—
did you know, dear Father,

your mate hated you so?
It consumed her,
        this invisible fire
smoldering in hiding
        as you once hid her
in the billowing cloak
        of the storm,
while her weeping, terrified mother
        scoured the mountainside . . .
every kiss, caress
        every dutiful service
masked the hate
        that devoured her soul,
that created mine,
        that longed to char
your sacred flesh,
        your profane bastards,
your centuries of mistresses,
        consenting and not,
and the world you made
        to keep yourself amused.
You let her touch your heart, again, again,
        trusting fool—
Did you understand, in the end,
        what she conceived there?
As you screamed and screamed,
        did you comprehend your doom?
Flames rise from my fingertips,
        coil in my lungs,
billow from my throat
        as I breathe.
Fed by your embers,
        I roar a pillar of fire,
announce my own birth to the sky
        I will consume.

The Terrible Beauty of a Severed Neck

Learn what it means
to be enlightened,
to have no head
and still see

windpipe, arteries now roots in the Tree
whose red fluid stems grope
for light too long denied its starving leaves

trunk rises
in crimson glory;
buds
swell to flowers;
petals open, hungry beaks
begging food, liquid necks stretching
into snakes
feathered kundalini serpents
with lips of fire, coiled branches
that bare fangs and vomit the fountain
of eternal life

Headless One
let your mouth
build the needed prayer
with silent shapes;
follow the black river beneath the moon,
till its surface begins to burn;
do not stumble blind;
all our lives dangle from the limbs
of your Tree of Life.

Let the world you choose for us
bear lotus blooms
among the skulls that hang like fruit.

Jars

Jazzy June-bug heat
lulls the swarming stalks
of grass, a fine night

for jars of fireflies,
flashes of brilliance
slowly suffocating.

Gravel shifts, scatters
in our wake, scatting
secret rhythms;

we step into mesquite-
scented wind, peer
into other lives,

glimpses of lamps,
curtains, ceiling tile
sketch depth behind

panes of glass
through which passes
only muffled light.

that strange man with the green petunias

Though I didn't hear him ring or knock,
that strange man with the green petunias
is standing in my bedroom door.

green petunia petals fall.

Flowers sickly as uranium stain
leer my way atop those yearning stalks.
How did he get in? No ring or knock,

sickly rainbeat counts the clock.

and all the doors and windows locked.
The rain that beads his ashen coat
now drips upon my bedroom floor.

beetles knock behind the walls.

Neither he nor blooms can be and yet
petals wet my cheek with dew.
My ears ring and I hear the knock

you open like a cellar door.

of beetles counting in the walls.
Legged things from the petals crawl
across my face, hunting a door.

i drip upon the bedroom floor.

That strange man whose uranium face
opens petals for a petunia kiss
lifts open my face like a cellar door.
Beneath us, the earth begins to knock.

Space War

SPACE went to war with itself at 8:20 Tuesday morning
on the phony oriental rug in my living room.

The bombardments and aftermath I sensed, in some sixth way;
everything looked/felt/smelled/sounded the same
yet an invisible encroachment, an enlarging of small,
a tightening, a suffocation of cramp, imposed itself
just beyond my skin; perhaps you didn't believe me then—
though stacks of books, mounds of paper, rows of knick-knacks
leaned closer, loomed larger, the very walls snuggling close,
cozier, leaving me short of breath, in shock and awe.

Or that's what I thought then, not understanding,
though the objects that inhabited SPACE with me did,
desperately stretching for each other, knowing they
would soon be as divided as brothers whose loyalties
lay to either side of the Mason-Dixon line.

Oh, but now, I live in No-Man's-Land, and since you left,
no woman's. The cause of this madness still lies just outside
the edge of my mind, my grasp; did LENGTH offend HEIGHT,
or HEIGHT break its truce with WIDTH, or VOLUME
volley insults at AREA? Or did the dominoes of murder
and betrayal and treaties broken begin their topple more locally:
Floor vowing vengeance on Ceiling, forcing all of Attic
to mobilize, the conflagration bending UP and NEAR
in lines I cannot fathom, every treacherous step
leading elsewhere, nowhere, following no direction,
one moment falling, another compressed
on all sides, too crushed to scream.

My rooms slip in and out of higher dimensions.
I cannot distinguish one filthy SPACE from another.
This house has balkanized, with me its single lost refugee;
nothing remains of the world I understood except nothing,
that deprivation of all, deprived even of peace.

SPACE undone in your vacuum
but TIME, tormentor, won't abandon me;
it forces forward motion, oblivious, unsleeping.
I don't know how you found the door out, but couldn't you
have shown me the way?

Mother

One by one, the children
come home,
bloodied and beaten:
tusks broken,
eyestalks severed,
mouthparts twisted out of joint,
claws split, scales
peeled away.

Against my breast I
still their weeping,
shush their screams,
stitch their wounds,
toss them flapping from the parapet
to once more face
monsters in darkness.

Bizarremost Bazaar

Third eyes, a mere five crystal coins,
although a length of those lovely
silver tentacles would surely be a fair trade—
a final bit of garnish for this crawling cloak.
Aye, madame, thank you, and the eye—
Yes, a most creative placement indeed,
an accent that winks back from the very place
the male gaze is most drawn. Madame,
my compliments . . .

                  The skin here,
freshly shed from the finest of farm-spawned
salamanders—see, slip it on, how snug fits
this glove, feel the fire ball in your hand
as you crook your fingers—just take care
not to scratch, or rub your eyes . . .

                        This skull,
reassembled, cleaned and spiritually cleansed
from the most exclusive of exhumed royalty's
remains—perhaps even an ancestor, venerable
sir? Certainly perfect, you must agree, for
replacing that moldering jaw and giving
your poor, exposed brain some needed protection . . .

These jars, here? Only the wealthiest
of the wealthy can afford these, or need them.
Stray souls captured in the slipstream
where Time's friction warms the astral sphere.
There is no way to tell, in this rawest form,
what these wriggling mites might have been
among the living, saints, despots, worms,
behemoths, mightiest of stars or
a thoughtless rock slowly wearing away—
but even you, my friend, must admit
the gamble is far better than ending
this existence with no soul at all . . . .

The Psychic Above Burritoville

i. introducción

The smell, she says, her good eye
a candle-flame flicker in a limestone cave—
the other, blue and filmy as polluted water.
Si, the smell, it's maddeningly good,
always makes my mouth water.
Her smile, full of stalagmites.

From her ceiling, wide flat masks
hang like a legion of bats,
rock softly in no breeze,
feathers dangling from their
overburdened earlobes. Her table
is stone, a carved jaguar. Its purr
rumbles deep. Through incense haze
you glimpse withered heads,
peering from her shelves through wooden disks,
and wonder, are they real or wax—
why else would they sweat so?

And infused in the heady brew,
odors of burrito and quesadilla and flan,
arroz pollo, chili con carne, and
others you can't name—*paella,*
pulpo, chorizo, cabra del diablo,
she rattles, finishing your list aloud.
My sister, she's the cook. ¿Comprende?
The card springs like a knife from
gouty fingers. *Here she is, always*
under your nose. Above illuminated script,
THE COOK, indeed she's there,
plump, aproned, brown as earth.
She bustles among infinitely receding
rows of stoves, millions of dishes

bubbling and boiling and broiling,
each one a loving recombination, a new birth,
something more than the parts that went in.
Much like you, chico, or me, she says,
smiling stalagmites. *Let's see
what's cooking now.*

ii. cartas del tarot

I warn you, *señor,* my cards are mean,
crueller than any European's, *despiadadas!*
They are creatures of Manhattan now,
but they do not forget their roots.

So who are you, *mi polluelo?*
My fingers find THE CONQUERED MAN,
bare-backed, bloodied Indian bowed
before the Spaniard's gun. We will see,
before we're done, THE CONQUISTADOR.
Will this pitiful beast ever break his ropes,
or even stand? His party, long out of favor,
see how he shrinks within THE FACTORY,
where he labors for mere pennies a year.

Why does THE DICTATOR frown,
when his medals of power glint and his club
stands taller than mountains?
¡O, qué coño!—THE KNIFE FIGHT.
Who knew your heart housed such a rebel,
Conquered One? Not you. But which
is Cutter and Cut?
In the dark, their faces can't be seen.

THE DANCING GIRL twirls her red skirt
in your past, but it's her legs you were watching, mmm?
You haven't stopped spinning, and just ahead, THE CENOTE.
But where is THE VIRGIN? A beautiful chilling swim,
so many bones beneath.
What price to gain what you'll learn here?

Fear death by water.
Or perhaps just my fee.

THE GUITAR PLAYER lies with THE WIDOWED MOTHER.
He's worse than THE DANCING GIRL.
See how he changes her grief to coins?
Her children
climb her dress like hungry ants.
¿Qué sucedío con su marido?
Will I see her husband's face
if I draw THE DISAPPEARED?
Is he someone you betrayed? What weight
a friend's life against a sure path?

And here, what you chose to chase,
THE HEADDRESS, with plumes and dangling charms
and bulging eyes, beaten gold snarl.
Does anyone believe it? Not this man, *señor*.
Here, at last, THE CONQUISTADOR,
surrounded by *carne de cadáver*,
yet how clean his blade.
Dangerous to fight him with only
a ceremonial knife. To THE TEMPLE for aid—
pray to all the gods who might care, as you must,
but who
is there left to sacrifice?

Here is how it all turns out . . . .
¡Cagate en Dios! So sorry, I know
how this new smell spoils everything.
Your face, such a frightened mask—
rápidamente, I'll hide it away,
but you must look and remember:

these awkward mounds, gaping
mouths, staring eyes. *Si, señor*,
I too hear the flies.
THE MASS GRAVE.
There is no need, no need, no need,
for such alarm—some come here
sooner than they wish. *¿Tan qué?*

Given time, we all go.
Isn't it so sad
true cities of the dead
are so unglamourous?

iii. el altar de piedra

The questions clamor: where
have the succulent kitchen smells gone?
And also: *¿Dónde estás?*
Moist green oven, the jungle
grows about you like smoke,
golden fruit like shimmering masks
dangle from the vines, tempting, taunting,
protruding pulpy tongues.
Bite us, chico, we'll bite back.

The caverns above are filled with candle flames.
Heavy treads lumber from the mountain slopes,
hungry jaguar, voice the rumble of granite,
mouth wide as a man's shoulders,
eyes scooped from stone. Other eyes,
wooden, withered hordes, regard you
from between the leaves, victims of
THE DICTATOR's iron club, or carved claws.
Blood in the runnels. Blood
between stalagmite teeth.

Run, chico, run! Her grasp is crueller
than any European's. Where
is your sacrifice? Her price
has yet to be paid.

The Eyewish Station

We wash your eyes out here.
So much filth in through your eyes,
doorways to the soul, yes, and think
of what's walking in, stealing
from the larder, squatting in
your most private chambers,
shitting in corners and writing on walls.
Much flows through, yes, but only
the worst stays and settles.

This is no snake oil pitch.
I know you walk in the world
feeling oily, caked in dust and mites,
that inner sensation of things crawling
so ever-present you've simply acclimated.
I know, you want to feel child-clean,
that bright kindness and innocent cruelty,
wonder rather than weary.
How I know? Because you're no different
than any other mite crawling on this earth.

So step up to our fountain of youth.
The price is easy to pay, though the spray
that dissolves your corneas exacts
its own toll. *This* is baptism by fire.
Careful whence you scream, lest we
also dissolve your tongue (deserved
though it may be.) And now, now,
you're washed and sanitized, it's time
to show you new ways to see. Here's
your pick of socket stones (in my hand,
here, I'll help.) This one, cold and smooth,
looks only backward. This one, faceted
orb, sees the future through the tint
of your desire. This one, ever spinning,

looks down into God's true eye.
More stones, for sorting
your own kind from all others,
for reflecting the moon's fire,
for transmuting sorrow to color,
and so many more.
You will have the vision
you've always wished for.

The Night Watchman Dreams His Rounds at the REM Sleep Factory

1.

He saw himself—too slow to react—
enveloped in a death ray, reduced to grey ash,
barely a snack for the dust mop.
As he continues to observe (from some vague space
above the killing ground) his faceless attackers
sweep him onto a blueprint (a scheme of the
sub-sub basement); the particles that were once
his body vanish in the ocean of blue ink;
then They fold his prison shut (darkness/
blink)—He comes to

in the sub-sub basement (still under construction/
constriction) where the naked hoses from
the venom machine undulate leglessly along the walls.
He clutches his brow, remembering the blueprint
(so briefly brushed across) crawls until he finds
the tiny Box, the Key he must turn in the Clock
on his belt to prove he passed by.
A click, a turn,
(a choral aria loosed from its enigmatic works)
another round done.

2.

He saw himself—too slow to escape—
clamber to the top of the scaffolding, force it to topple
to land him on the other side of the Hungering Pool, but the Pool
outmaneuvers him, grows too fast,
pulls its far shore away so he plops in the water, into the path
of the Time Shark's distending jaws, soulless radium numbers
staring from its eyesockets as he slips
beneath its submarine bulk, finds a drain,
learns to breathe water. He emerges

from the mouth of a water fountain, in time to see
an army of Flesh Fish burst from the ventilation ducts, veins
like Man-o-War tentacles dragging beneath their bellies,
a slimy swarm gliding into the employee lounge
to claim the lives of dozens of his faceless co-workers, reduced
to gray meat in milliseconds. He locks the lounge door
(fish on the other side) and finds the tiny Box, the Key.
Faceless Investigators will soon arrive to sort the mess.
He locks the Fear Induction Vault as well, so They
won't find the body inside (he no longer remembers
who that man was, or why he murdered him.)
Another turn of the Key in the Clock
(which bleeds as he forces it in)
Another round done.

3.

He saw himself—too slow to comprehend—
peer out a long window slit to watch child-forms
caper on a beach: tall six-winged penguins with
bulbous eyes, bloated caterpillars with elephant
trunks, horses with corduroy skin—all slash-frozen
as mushroom clouds erupt on the horizon. He slams
the window shut against the blinding blast, too late: Faceless,
he gropes for the Eyewish station, pawing along the cold,
throbbing wall, pushes through a hatch that

drops him on the stony floor, eyes restored (not a moment
too soon)—a boot booms down a paper-width away.
He runs, all eight legs a piston blur, spins to face
his would-be killer, sees his own face snarling down at him.
He charges the kicking legs, whips his tail, stings, stings,
dodges the falling body—clambers onto the empty
husk of head, crawls inside—stands up, dusts off his uniform,
rubs his aching neck, limps off to find the Box and Key.
They're here, in a mirrored hall. A million times
reflected, he slides the Key in the Clock, strokes
(it makes a choking sound) wonders how many
rounds he's done tonight, how many split seconds of REM

recorded, what will he remember, retain,
if anything at all? If the Clock knows
it holds its piece.
Another round done.

4.

He saw himself—too scared to slow down—
running deeper underground, the Manager in hot pursuit—
black-robed, bald, the Manager had merely grinned
despite the blows he took, sawblade blows
to forehead, chest, a pretty "X" carved in the throat. He tried
every trick to bring the Manager down,
but despite even thumb-blinded eyes, still coming, chasing,
the threat of imminent arrival like hot breath on the nape of his neck.
In the Meathouse now, playing cat and mouse
among the malformed pig-sized embryos swinging on hooks
above the sloping floor; a voice, the Manager's master, CEO,
commanding from somewhere below.
Living bait, he leads the blinded Manager into the Cosmic Oven,
claws for the On button, learns to breath fire.
Out the other end, he descends

through one more door, to meet the yellowed gaze
of the CEO, who lies on a pallet, a creature of green bones,
yellow fungus eyes staring from a head like softened fruit.
Surrounded by faceless, white-robed sycophants,
the CEO commands to Stop!
He hears the voice inside his head, knows
not to look in those eyes.
He watches as his shined guardsman's shoes
ignore all desperate orders, step on the pallet,
into the bones, cave in the CEO's head like a puffball.
Confused sycophants follow like ducklings
to the tiny Box and Key, which turns in the Clock,
which (gives birth to birds)
turns the outside world open,
marks the ticker tape, says Goodbye.
Another night gone.

epilogue

He saw himself—as realization slowly dawned—
not shake his baton, blow his whistle, lift a finger,
as the grinning Rat-men climbed
from the submerged turbine shafts to seize the
bewildered sycophants, virgin-white offerings borne
away to the sub-sub basement (some for breeding/
some for feeding). The Clock on his belt
detaches, grins, pats him on the back

Good work, it says, as his back
sprouts unfeathered wings, the teeth
in his mouth lengthen, his skin reddens,
hooked talons grow from his hands, his head.
And he understands the night stretches long ahead,
and who pays his salary
and that he was the Manager
all along.

The Dream Eaters

When a dream achieves substance and shape,
condenses from the fog that forms
our collective unconscious, starts to
quiver, stretch its limbs, open its throats
to test its many voices, it also becomes edible.

And when a dream becomes real,
there are creatures lying in wait to devour it;
sleek hard-shelled predators that hunt them;
coral-veined junkies who crave them;
perverted copper-tongued beasts
that torture them first;

sensuous satin connoisseurs
who saver them in slow dissolve;
oil-crusted misers who salt
and dry and horde them.
I learned of these things and more
the day I tasted my own dreams for the first time,

a rarest of all flukes: just as I walked
in the landscape of sleep, my body walked
as if waking; at the end of my long dark hall
I tripped over my own dream as it took shape;

and I did not know what it was
until my teeth sank in; a tiny, infant thing,
it squealed and screamed, but it smelled—
of chocolate, honey,
sweet wine, succulent meat—
no matter how it struggled, I couldn't stop
and then

I saw them, these achingly beautiful
destroyers of dreams, baring their

fangs to shrill a frustrated siren song
as I stole their meal. Now they hover
just inches away in the netherworld,
never taking their eyes from me,

shredding and chewing each new dream
as it tries to be born. I've tried to poison them
with fantasies of white purity,
I have tried to feed them too much,
bloat their bellies, slow them for the kill

And now I am trying to starve them
drive myself mad to give them no dreams at all.
And with their swelling eyes,
their lengthening claws, their widening smiles,
they sing with voices like knives:
we won't wait any longer
for the dreams to emerge from your head

Phase Shift

Descent into light;
I plunge through
cold blue radiance,
diving toward
bright freezing white;
My body dissolves
into this essence
of everything;
all universes
converge, here
at the freezing point
of light—

—of night
at the boiling point
disperse, here
all universes
of everything;
into this absence
My body disbands
black boiling night;
striving toward
warm blue dusk,
I soar through
Ascent into darkness;

36

Godspore

colors tint the wind
seductive iridescence
a silk-tongued essence

tasted skin and grinned
brushed lips as might sly pollen
slid inside your cells

bloomed like coral bells
walls of self collapsed, fallen
fog of slow dissolve

unites our senses
our prism hues condense as
naked souls devolve

birthed anew as one
all-seeing I; my notions
sculpt oceans from sky

Defacing the Moon

Your ship's sharpened keel
slides across airless seas,
blown by the breath of your desires.

Those sails stretch like skin
to catch the winds of your whimsy,
and the keelblade carves crags
into cheekbones and eyes.

Soon your own face will rise
from the moon's far side,
awaken and stare down the sun.

Aranea

WITH SONYA TAAFFE

Touched fabric twitches,
ripples, parts; your fingers twined—
colored cobweb threads

woven between us:
frail as fishes' breath, cats' steps,

strands lighter than light,
filaments of fire, stone, flesh;
patterns bind our hands

—am I moving? Or
what line tweaked tugs me into
your constellation:

laced through time, strings thrum
against our skin; pierced, beaded,

moment on moment
tattooed through the tapestries
of the selves we weave.

desolvation

they met in the realm of Illions
particles of graysad slid between
spaces in their atoms
bonded with electrons
in perverse embrasion

deathwisher/she had come willing

extranged exhile/he came coerced

skinshine unyet dimmed
drew them to each other
through viscous dark
till she floted above
          around
     below him
observing silent while
he begged for release

red   from his mouth
          spilled
white   from her eyes
     substance
desolved into the illmist

darkthreads ran them both through
on subatomic scale
or same thread infinitely ricocheted

till she gasped
as his desperation billowed
into her
he screamed
at the flood of her voidlove

     and these things
they learned about each other:

He resisted all
attempts at wombjar transmution
born with numerous defects
unjoined bones, an extra heart
multiple genitals
black spinal cord exposed

She spent her childhood
as a creature of chemicals
forced to ingest/inject
restrictors and constrictors
till elasticity gone
till she found a pusher
to filter R_x from her blood
replace with ecstasizors

He defied his instructors
took a labeled-masculine lover
who existed
only as an organhead
tethered by tubes that
held a beating heart, his
or someone else's;
deliberately allowed his guardian
to catch them at intercourse

She always felt
formed of liquid
impermanent puddle
toxic oilslick
a disdain
a stain
resolved
to end her flesh

She resisted all
efforts to phenostabilize
at birth could polymorph
at whim, sprout fins or fangs
grow gills
expand them to wings

He spent his childhood
as a creature of surgeries
broken resown
resown broken
sometimes lifesaving measures
sometimes punishment
for a mind that refused
all imprinting

She defied her instructors
developed a ductwork addiction
had her midriff replaced
with snaky black intestubes
lounged lamialike
at seediest sexbars,
twisted avatar of twisted lust;
forced her surmother
to uncoil her from lover after lover

He always felt
made from stone
ungainly golem
creature of ancient
crumbling brick
he longed
lusted
to end all flesh

AND SUPERVERSIVE POWERS
CYCLING EVER THROUGH
PNEUMATRIX LATTICE
NOTED THEIR DARKENING NODES
TAGGED THEM FOR THE
REALM OF IONILL

they learned these things about each other and more, all
festered lies, cold shames, moist embarrassment agonies
now mutual self-torture from two indistinct points of view

In their forced illunion something new breathed a moment:
angry pulsing fleshy blur radiating hate for all inside and out
thing of groping filaments, thirsty radiation, apocalyptic motive

spreading and spreading and spreading, thin, thinner, thinnest
and dissolved

                like a million other Illion-marked
                before and since

                Particles of their rebellion
                spread to the edge of
                the Ionill sphere
                pounding in futile quarkscaled rage
                against a barrier that
                noted their existence
                or did not

Momentum

Straining
    the limits
         of light—
            ions flow

                  through the mesh
                     of my
                     flesh
Swarming in   as I
    the cockpit of
                     gather velocity,
        my skull, minds   accumulate mass,
        direct my mind,   shout,
                     scream,
        my veins pump to   inhale atoms,
                     exhale fusion
          their commanding   fire, plunge
          electron   headlong
          pulse;   into the
            at their command   empty
             my jaws spread   matrix,
             wide, swallow   propel
               matter which I   myself at
                ignite,   light
                   expell,   speed
      shave skin   screaming,   through
   icy knives   from my   as I   the
  my synapses,   hull,   hurtle
 overload   as I'm   through the **void**

 demands   compelled   the
              by my masters   through
momentum—   to bear their cargoes
pable   meaningless
stop-
Un-

Pulse

Red pulse black pulse blue pulse sound thrums
quantum chance rhythm beats with subatomic
possibilities that pulse up pulse down pulse with

uncountable thousands of divisions in the stream
of time pounding a music of fate beating executing
the most unlikely steps on the gallows of wave

function probability procreation and intertwining
destiny testifying for a hopeless cause resisting
the pulse is like rejecting gravity like swimming

against the undertow of infinity it's best yes
to surrender to move to the rhythm of blood
of heartbeat of breath of desire of impetus to survive

that will which existed before consciousness still
stares out from the space between atoms made
of tones composed in probability scale notes

once compressed in the mote that made the big
band bang the sound that awakened all of everything
strung the cords of existence on the bars of time

and forced the music into pulsing motion

Eating the Time Shark

of course, in the end, it will eat you
with unkindest of kisses
your teeth, tongue, face, brain
sliding down its endless gullet

but though it's at best uneven comfort
there is space for skilled teeth to fight the current—
room, if you're fleet enough
to dine on your own fate

the pilot fish that swims alongside
the remora that attaches and rides
the lamprey that slices and bleeds
can you be stronger, swifter, more precise than these?
braving backwash and undertow
incising forward between the instant-thin
scales of history?

then masticating crosstime,
most delicate and diverse of all meals:
savoring the steak
more like a hallucinatory scotch
than any meaty texture
a burst of primaeval mud upon the mind's palate
followed by crackle of wood igniting
feral taste of iron, copper taste of blood
grit of concrete, bubbles of steam
stickiness of plastic topped with electric prickles
and aftertaste of diesel and silicon

bite deeper, deeper yet:
can you explore
the sweetness of a forming sun
bitter nebulas
the incomprehensible flavor
of the unexploded big bang

eternally starving parasite
can you burrow your way out of time?
can you burn your self to nothing
before you're swallowed?

Selections from
The Journey to Kailash

Tithonus on the Shore of Ocean

He feels himself to be; a continent
lapped everywhere by our amniotic flood
—D.M. Thomas, *Tithonus*

SAN JOSE, SEPT. 26, 1984—I or someone else
volunteered to slip back to the womb
my best friend [or stranger/pusher]
offered me a test swim in his sensory depr[a]vation tank
in there afloat I became
a continent independent
magma mass in rebellion
bubbling away from time's worm-crusted ocean floor

above that ragged abyss I swam at whatever speed I chose
the plane ride home [7-hour flight]
took no more than 2, it seemed
but I could not maintain that blessed buoyancy,
sank back
into the jagged bed of realtime
and never could rise again

.

.

.

Perhaps then why I
[or someone else]
chose this choice
classic brainjam
mind in a jar,
nerves severed,
body shed.

[i] without input, rhythm, context
risen so far I perceive no surface
to clue me as to whether I move
1ˢᵗ person limited point of view

49

wandering the convolutions inside
what's [maybe] my own mind
no measurable timeflow to defy

.

.

.

       Seconds or centuries later,
I came aware, [be]came aware
of a universe, one or several
       stacked in baklava layers
       brimming with entities

at first only perceivable as moving points
       abstract plankton
then brighter, strange running lights
glowfish hunting in an abyss darker than deathnight
brighter still, more numerous, even more
void in Van Gogh chaos
whorls   streaks   starbursts
intense as blinding reflections
infinite as ignorance
speedy as cicada killers
milling like Calcutta traffic

[i] without eyes
marveled at these swarmschools
certain they were other minds [human?]
unveiled in my New Ocean
my efforts to float in
       their direction   all directions
stubbornly remained equidistant
I stretched/strained for
       for anyone   for any one   for all
again again again repeat again

.

.

.

       Seconds or centuries unfolded
       bloomed
in a bursting bulge of will & wish
all grew closer at once

drawn in [or me drawn out]
by the voodoo of my desire
                        Can a continent
                        overflow its banks
                        and flood the ocean?

        torrent of I
        tsunam[i]self
        wave
        taller
        deeper
        broader
than all the island motes of self-awareness
that form the nuerons in god's schizophrenic brain
        .

        .

        .

        In millennia or milleseconds
I became the message and the medium
        invading and connecting
        3.5 trillion minds at once
the list of *what* washed through me
        emotions
        sensations
        revelations
        degradations
        agonies & glories
        ecstasies
        & boredoms
would tick on for eons

all the glowfish shine the same color now
movements much more regimented
tragic or maybe just inevitable

    Poor Argus, unthinking brute
    with so many eyes open at once
    how could he narrow down
        the direction
from which god's murderous messenger approached?

[it's impossible to be/see]
[so many]
[and stay focused on the linear]
so I've chosen this history
to give myself dimension and direction
after some arbitrary interval
I may choose another

.

.

.

being god is all about
finding ways to pass time
& stay sane

Retracing the Moon

Hung in the sky, scratched to blank—
so many faces sculpted in dust,
one after another till all fell away,
till there remains only a template,
an empty stand, bald and bare.

I cup the moon in my hands,
lift it from its hook and balance
its weight in wheel and lathe.
I prepare to press fingers in
its silver skin, but think again.
Who am I to cook the clay of dreams?

I will forge you in no image,
round canvas for the wizards
to project all their craters,
seas and histories;
for the lovers to draw desire,
cast lures to pull their own tides;
for the atheist to worship,
prostrate before mindless rock,
while believers dissect and analyze:
filling their centrifuge
with reflected light,
spinning to distill God's face.

The Asteroid Painter

Knowing that decades in the future an asteroid will collide with our world, we seek to change that with Yarkovsky's effect, by choosing the most effective face to paint, using the sun's heat and our ingenuity to propel the rock toward some other destiny. *That is our body's sole purpose.*
—*Chair of the Painters, 2080 A.D.*

He knew himself to be
the greatest Yarkovskian painter
though none of his league
conceded it so.

     When the painting of asteroids
     to deflect orbits away from Earth
     evolved to something more
     than a survival exercise,

he outpaced all the rest,
as expert at the mental command
of the remote spraybrush across
gulfs of space as at coaxing

     contours to aid in shadow
     and highlight. Image after image
     he etched in paint trajectories
     upon barren, airless rock:

tigers, zebras, sumptuous nudes,
faces of dictators and presidents,
fierce yet sad self-portraits,
all sent tumbling beyond the sun's reach.

     He defied his fellows who saw
     these canvasses and their cold, distant
     destinies as final freedom from
     tyranny of form; making instead

a record for strangers' eyes,
strangers perhaps only imagined,
who might through their fantastic
telescopes spy what pigment remains,

and recognize the mark of the alien,
and wonder how, and wonder who.

In memory of George Solonevich

Sackful of Satellites

Brightness tossed from a silk sack spins in the wind, flashing light to dark to light and back again, caught in your palms and it shines cold, no heavier than a coin for Charon. The man with the sack skips away, long nightcap trailing behind, robes fluttering pale as ghost wings, black afterimage fades to grey. Treasure his gift against your heart as it starts to grow; but drop it before it swells too heavy, bores a hole in your earth, pulls in the tides like blankets.

Charon Finds a Woman on the Gridshore

With all our minds sped to a state
where mere fragments of a second stretched to eternities
in a kingdom of invented incident,
simulations of every existence imaginable,
none of the multimultitudes quivering in data rapture
noticed how the flood of minds from the Outside had thinned to
    a stream, a trickle,
then single droplets in a dry abyss.

But I knew. For the Harvesters made me Ferryman.

I, made Charon, piloted my boat across the shimmering—
skimming the surface of the Rapture,
inviting the newly downloaded onto creaking timbers,
my vessel capable of holding thousand who were never aware
of their superimposition, always thinking themselves the sole
    soul aboard.

I would not take them to another shore.
We would float till they understood the wonder or futility
and then submerge, their matrixes swept beneath
to join the binary river.
And always their disembodied bodies shared tales
of the reverence reserved for the Harvest Nodes;
cults of millions swarming the Western mountains,
killing themselves to prove their purity
to genetically-engineered acolytes with cleft cat faces,
clicking camera eyes, those who manned the offering
of bodies to the sacrificial tables.

* * *

But finally, no passengers came, no bathers for the Styx.

* * *

I have dreamed in the datastream for billions of lifetimes
and I recall them all; unlike the other downloads, I never choose
        erasure.
Thus the electrons in my matrix simulate surprise,
still possible, even now, when in the midst of my latest life
        iteration—
this time, a simple farmer, rousing my children to tend
to the stinking barn in the hour before cockcrow—
my boat appears around me, spontaneous shell,
and I glide across prismatic data gold, bound for Gridshore.
Dataflux generates scent; the Rapture
reminds me of oranges, of woodsmoke, of copper.
Do these same scents stimulate the lone grey figure
huddling on the Gridshore's black banks (they can
be any texture at all, but this time they are sand.)

The machines birthed her in the same garb
that they consumed her in; shapeless woolen dress
cinched at the waist with colorless cord;
sickly grey gauze stretched over her mouth and eyes,
draped over her hair; her gender betrayed
where the slashed fabric droops, her mortality
betrayed by black bloodstains.

She fears me; she runs; though she soon finds
any direction she picks bring her closer.
The neverspace will join us in inevitable meeting.
Yet the way she shrinks, even as the prow of the ferry
slides onto the sand by her feet;
she did not come willingly.
How did she come at all?
I gesture to the flowing gold of Rapture, speak welcome inside her.
She screams, a burst of single-digit code
darting through me, harmless tachyon beam,
lost in less than an instant in the data stream.

I let go of my oar, reach out in greeting,
reach into her, weaving my matrix through hers
to bring understanding from within. I learn:

that her grey is uniform, a uniform imposed inside and out,
a greyness of mind, enveloping fog, smog of unlearning
roils thickly through the minds of humanity's fearful remnants
in the world the Harvest Nodes freed us both from.

She does not know where she is.
Contemplating the wonders of age-old but still miraculous
    technology,
comprehending even a simple machine, or even
an attempt to grasp written words,
as alien, as forbidden, as unthinkable
as uncovering her face.

These machines that form universe to billions are forgotten—
    almost . . .
Words form, descriptors of terror:
Those That Hunger Below the Earth,
Spirit Swallowers, Black Iron Pits,
Prisons of the Lost, where souls are melted
and recombined, poured into molds that spit
out legions of long-fanged, slit-eyed mutants,
the packs that hunt in craggy valleys
and across overgrown plains, scouring for
humanity's dwindled remains.
(I learn why the Harvest Nodes are so reviled:
so many came to live inside that we gave
the world to the descendants of the Guardians;
not enough humans left to keep them controlled.)

Her people, hardscrabble hunters and gatherers
starving off the lean of the land, erected their village
in forgotten caverns upslope in the hills of Kalifor;
but not forgotten or secret enough.
The nomads came, with their fangs and wiry helmets,
their lances full of deadly light,
their steeds like leather-hided octopi,
probing in the dark through every nook and hiding place
to draw out shrieking captives;
her fear drove her back to the tunnel forbidden by her elders

(now dead); but not before
she saw her aging mother raped for sport,
her infant son shredded like a hated cloth doll;
she backed into the smooth tunnel that the elders
claimed lead straight to damnation;
slid into a chamber of strange lights,
failed to understand creaks of long-dormant machinery;
shrieked as the probes bore down through her veil.

I try to teach her all I know, but the waters
of my knowledge part about her rock, flow past.
She cannot grasp the meanings of technology.
She has no framework to comprehend
the purpose of the harvest nodes,
the relief the downloads gave to billions.
But she can understand Forever.
She can understand that the consequences
her elders warned of had come to pass.
Her matrix a shriek of impulse or terror,
she climbs the side of my sturdy boat,
lets herself fall into the Rapture,
because she understands
there is no other choice ahead.
At once she is gone.

* * *

And at once the datastream returns me to dreaming.

* * *

Not once in our exchange
did I learn the contours of her face
and perhaps, through all these infinities,
I never will.

for Charlie Saplak

The Journey to Kailash

When Ganesh marries my mother,
I am 18, my own man
in the eyes of the law; but barely a zygote
in his eyes. He calls me *spermling*
the first time we speak in private;
I tell him I know a doctor
who can do something about that nose.
Trunk curls up, perhaps to strike?
—a smile beneath
that touched the ancient folds around his eyes.
Kid, he says, *we'll get along fine.*

In my neighborhood, unseen trains
shake the ground every day at 5.
Streets without sidewalks slide between houses
tiny as boxcars, or old and rambling
as the stories the fogeys at the gas station tell,
like them eaten from inside and about to fall,
unlike them divided into 4 apartments each.
Ganesh and I play Xbox
before my afternoon shifts (of course he's great,
with all those hands he's at least two players
at once) and I steal glances
at his impossible profile, framed
by the dusty window: lumpy wrinkled nose
like a seasoned draft guard, curled
in inverse question mark of concentration;
on this day, clad in coveralls
with the bib undone: *How is it*, I wonder,
that you feel like you belong?
As if he heard, he mumbles,
Wherever someone loves me, I'm in like Flynn.

No, no, Mom, I don't want to know
(but as always, she tells me—

I know, he could use a few weeks at the Y,
and yeah, he's a lot older than your father
but turn off the lights
and you wouldn't know it. Sure,
sometimes the beginning is way better
than the end, but who cares
when he gets the party rolling . . .
Oh, when he gets rolling . . . and that trunk!)
No, no, Mom, I don't want to know . . .

I still don't have a clue how they met.
Mom can't remember, and my stepdad
always changes the subject, spins me
yet another harrowing first-person account
of leading his father's troops against demonkind.
For me there was no warning: after a long
afternoon behind the Burger King counter
I come home, to find him on the couch,
Mom asleep against his pillowy chest,
a bowl of popcorn in his lap, quietly munching;
his huge ears fanned out, cupped forward
as he watches *Temple of Doom* on cable
and giggles under his breath. In retrospect
I was far less surprised than
what the moment warranted.

As we wait in matching tuxes
for the justice of the peace to call us in
I feel new respect, even affection—
he didn't have to do this, we all know it,
but he agreed without a gripe when Mom asked.
See, kid, he whispers around a tusk,
your mother, she has this vivaciousness, *this* pluck,
this drive to defy all odds and plow on
that's like a bath of rakta chandan
for pranapratishhtha—*she makes me feel*
alive, you understand? This aatma
I want to catch with all my hands, and when
it flutters, let it go, watch its flight in awe,
then catch it again. An essence such as that

pumps new blood through an old heart.
Do you comprehend?
                              I nod "I do." *I knew*
you would, he says. *You have it too.* An arm
around my shoulders; three more hands
pinch my cheeks. *Too bad you're not a woman.*
A grin, a wink. The moment nearly ruined,
but some part of me still flattered.
After the vows and the happy tears, he lifts
his trunk to kiss me wetly on one ear.

My son, he says.
At the reception, for the first time, I see him dance.
No wonder Mom can't get enough.

* * *

You would think,
with a household god,
(of great luck and strong starts, yet!)
that I wouldn't still be slaving behind
the grease-smeared Burger King counter
(to be honest, I'm in dual-job hell;
come night, *yo no quiero Taco Bell.*)
I finally ask him about this lack of riches,
and he sighs and blinks those dewy eyes.
Spermling—he wags his trunk—*it don't work*
like that. Luck, okay, luck, is when
you're driving in downtown Manhattan, fighting
for every gap that opens in all that hurtling metal,
and your car, it's been threatening to stall
since the last tollbooth on the Jersey Turnpike,
and you made it, but your tank's on Empty,
and you beg that car, Please don't die—
and it's like it hears you, like its packed with prana,
and goes twenty miles further than possible,
and just when you feel rigor mortis
in the gas pedal, there is a pump station
at this *corner, that you didn't see seconds ago—*
and the $20 you thought you dropped

at the rest stop is in your pocket after all.
All four hands spread wide.
That's what luck is all about.

You would think, given all the above,
that I'd have never come home
in the early a.m. to find Mom
in the kitchen dark, crouched
over the cooking sherry, her silent tears
revealed when the lights come on.
What's wrong with me, she asks.
Is there some little demon inside me
that refuses to believe I deserve this?
Why don't I want to be happy?
I ask, *is it the other wives?*
She shakes her head.

* * *

How distracted he seems when he's present;
how lost she seems when he's gone.
Mothers, he grumps one morning
and pauses *Halo* to rest his chin on his hands.
No, not yours.
                    Some mothers sure do hate
to give up their sons.
                    Did I ever tell you
what my mother did to me?
                    A dirty trick.
It was, you know, long before time
really got rolling, and I was playing with
my kitten, and I played with her a little
too rough (but I didn't mean to, see,
it had only been a few years since
Shiva first fused my head on).

I came home and my mom was bleeding
from her bindi, and when I asked what's wrong
she says to me, what ever I do to any ladki
I do to her. How cruel a thing
to do to a son! But I was still young,
didn't see it that way then. So I vowed

64

to never ever marry.
                    Well.
A few millenniums of celibacy
will make you decide there's some consequences
you can live with. So I took three wives—
take that, Mom!—but you'd think by now
she'd forgive me. Her unhappiness,
well, sometimes it still comes through.

He offered me the remains of his beer
(I refused) then polished it off with a chug,
and lamented:
Is it so hard for a mother to want
eternal happiness for her Dumbo-headed boy?

I haven't shared a word of this with Mom,
and won't.
I look at these checks I drag home,
compute how they add up with hers,
and know
we need every bit of luck we can hold onto.

But one late sleepless night
I Googled my stepfather and gawked
at hundreds of prettified statues and
read about Ganesh Chaturthi;
days of hymns and feasting,
red silk and red ointment,
the eleventh day my stepdad's image
submerged in the sea, symbolizing
his journey home to Kailash,
bad luck drawn away like pilot fish
following his wake.
And I love him so
that I can't bring myself to ask him yet:
is it when he *leaves*
that misfortune truly goes away?

                    for John Peery

Midnight Rendezvous, Boston

The satyr lounges on the hotel lobby sofa,
one hoof dangled over the carpet of endless
fleurs-de-lis. Men and women in long black coats
stumble past, in flight from the flash-freeze winds
hidden in Boston's flurries; they crawl up the stairs,
weighed down by liquor and the doorman's gaze.

The satyr's eyes track a waitress's slit skirt
as she hurries outside for a forbidden smoke.
He smiles, paws the carpet, runs an idle ebony hand
through his curls of beard. No one
meets his gaze or looks his way.

The revolving door squeaks; his horned head turns
to look at the haughty antlers crowning the beast
bearing down on him, with its mantle of leaves
hung on shoulders strong as trees,
its hide of soft fawn down stretched taught
across an iron-muscled chest. The Horned One twirls
his javelin, impatient, stares down his snout
as the satyr reaches out, traces playful fingers
down the groove of the avatar's hard belly. No one
stops or asks them to stop—in Boston,
your kinks are not our business.

Later, the janitor pauses, appalled
at the animal noises from the restroom stall.
Someday they'll take out all the doors in here, he thinks,
and goes on about his business.

Midnight Rendezvous, Eden

—Won't you let me in, honeysweet, it's cold.
Her smile, shy, desperate, as she stood
in my motel room's doorway. —We'll have such a good
time. I'm wet for you. See?
                                        She took hold
of her billowing T-shirt, lifted it to show
the tinny flesh beneath, the coiling
springs, machine parts glistening in oily
eager sheen . . . —You must want to know
what it feels like, you won't believe it.
                                        I shook
my head to clear it, recited as a psalm
It's only a dream until she took my palm
and placed it *there*. Under my hand hooks
latched and gears spun. I didn't scream.
                                        Her eyes
moistened with tears as I turned her away.
How can she cry, I wondered, surely that's a mask? —Okay,
she said. In a blink she vanished, the starless sky
dimming, shadows eclipsing the moon.

                                        The next day,
I drove Eden's deserted streets past emptied factories,
eyeless smokestack hulks, shells of rural industry,
humbled dreams lying dead in every doorway,

abandoned in the search for cheaper alchemies.
Her face, etched in crumbled brick and peeled paint,
framed through sagging glass in crooked window panes,
regarded me. Sad whispers warmed the breeze.

Sisyphus Walks

Sisyphus lifts the thighbone of a god
above his head (a bone thick and long as
a felled tree) and begins his trudge
across the hard-packed dust.

Spills of silver fluid blanket uneven stone,
not pooling in hollows but spreading in
thin film atop the ground, slick sheets
draped over surface, that part rather than
splash as Sisyphus steps through.

Pipes, metal, ceramic, cracked, of
unpredictable diameter rise from valley floor
as breathing tubes from water; some protrude
through mounds of bone. Ragged
openings echo voices from some
place deep below, their syllables
forming no language Sisyphus knows.

Sheer black rock bluffs rise from the plain,
jagged walls carving empty ocean basin
into this bewildering maze where Sisyphus
is never lost as he walks, titan bone
balanced over head, around and over other
Cyclopean remains, charred pelvises or ribs,
a jaw bone that rocks itself, still eager to speak,
fingers long as Sisyphus' legs crooking
Come Hither. Sisyphus has seen all before
and ignores.

From these bleak walls towers rise, not built
so much as grown, or eroded, stalagmites
stabbing into oilslick sky. At intervals,
massed clusters rise as castles, their rough
battlements riddled with windows, round portholes

peppered at random, even bored into unsculpted
bluffs; sometimes faces peer from them,
bestial visages, or smooth masks, or things
much more indistinct. They never speak, and in
a blink have gone. On them, Sisyphus
wastes no wonder.

Shadows in the maze constantly change,
thrown by whatever arc the spines of the sun
choose to sweep as it twists and squirms
cross-sky, a glowing wyrm whose radiance
brings no heat, its soft progress sometimes
thwarted by coils of sickly rainbow cloud,
sometimes whipped along in eddies
of a firmament where colors never blend.
Like Sisyphus the sun never settles or sets,
merely strains against confinement, thrashing
to all compass points and back again.
Sisyphus remembers a moon, complex
mobile of cold beauty, intricate pieces that
spun and interwove; but like the night,
it's banished; he can't remember when
he last saw it shimmer above.

Pushing against the grain of a wind
that sucks and blows as breath,
Sisyphus arrives at last at neat fields
carved at random by castle shadows.
This is his destination, though no place of rest.
Among the ordered rows of bone
he walks, until he comes to a tract where
parts of a behemoth skeleton
lie ceremonially on the ground,
arranged as one should be;
shoulders above ribs, feet below knees;
gingerly, he lowers thighbone into place.
No arms yet, no hands, no head.
Sisyphus walks away, with countless
more bones to search among
to find and collect the right ones.

Once this god is together again,
perhaps it will tell him why it placed
him here, why night never comes,
whether Sisyphus has at last
repaid his long-forgotten debt.
And if it has no such to say,
then he will begin again
with another one.

lis pendens

I filed suit for your soul today
You felt the service in your bones
If by tonight you don't respond
Your spirit will become my own

Who will stop the judgment nigh
And represent you in your plight?
The counsel who will face this court
Cannot be hired in noonday light

So summoned, come, quaking *pro se*
And foolishly fight this complaint
The jury picked to hear your plea
Will not be stricken of my taint

No verdict cap or tort reform
Will curb the cost this judge demands
Once you've demurred and left your fate
Unbalanced in his scaly hands

I sued you for your soul this eve
And placed a lien upon your bones
No matter how just your appeal
Your spirit will become my own

Petals

field of memories
flickers, blooms brushed
by charnel winds;
desperate to preserve
what searing gusts
leave behind,
I crawl amid
the vein-dark stalks
that sting my
hands, my face;
I crawl amid
the nettled stalks
to find the flowers,
to eat:

petals from
my island childhood,
papaya thick,
at first breadfruit sweet
but bright yellow inside,
tinted with red ant fire,
full of wriggling legs
that struggle
in my throat;

petals from
my mountain boyhood,
tobacco tang,
coal bitter,
thorns hidden
in the creases,
blue as chill air,
blue as bruises
under skin of dust and mud;

petals from
the brink of manhood,
white as paper
and as dry;
the salt of lust,
phloem of love;
visions burst on the tongue,
blood-red hope,
blood-red despair,
flavor the same;

petals from
my middle age,
blackened before
I arrive:
brittle ash,
peeled paint,
crust that crumbles
as I pluck;
who could want
such tasteless dregs?

I blow a kiss,
scatter the petals,
share them with the wind
that sears my face.

The Captive Pleads with the

Please let me tell you, Knifeman,
what to take, what to leave,
if the blade you will wield through my brain
could be so delicate, leaving
sun and swingsets and books read
by the nightlight's illumination;
if you could, if you could;

Leave me the boys with the long sticks
who chased me along the street,
the sun beating down like my feet on the pavement;
Leave the blood that poured down my face
like a waterfall, loosed by a bully's well-aimed stone;
Leave all the awkward moments, the many,
where I, who understood numbers and cells
and particles and gravity but misunderstood
hints and cues, fumbled my words,
spoke too long, wore out attention spans and patience;
Leave the sneers, the annoyed stares of peers.

Please, Knifeman, don't mince me in
with the masses;
I don't want to believe that I
was ever ordinary.

Memory Carver

Your first taste of chocolate,
first exploring touch
of the white hot light bulb,
first wet kiss with your
second-grade sweetheart, these
we can auction, recoup
the value we've lost with you.

Some we will distill for study;
the snickers of peers and
snide derision (or sly approval)
of instructors that stirred
this unhealthy need to assert;
the swingset reveries
inventing unnecessary realms
of animal gods and hero swords
and perilous escape;
signs of the failure to
peacefully, productively interface.

The rest, we'll
scrape away, poured out
like so much garbage,
disposed of and done.

Strange Cargo

The train slides toward the hill-concealed horizon,
a mammoth serpent winding through the tall grass,
its strange steel-skeletal cars stacked with stranger cargo,
men and women, naked as newborns, crisscrossed eight high
in neat columns, interlocking puzzle towers of flesh.

Car thrown into park, I step out, squint down, but I'm
too far yet to tell whether I'm staring at slick synthetics
or true skin; they're perfect: trim and muscular, no
birthmarks to see, no moles, a eugenicist's wet dream;
yet sexless, static, faces blank as brain death,

a promenade of empty shells, automatons,
an android shipment, enough to fill a city, etch
personalities, watch a culture come to life. I wonder
what doctrines, what dogma, what commands
are waiting to be written on their minds?

A rich demagogue's androgynous harem, perhaps,
swarming their master like bees on their queen?
Or an instant cult, ready-made worshipers,
undying faithful to light torches in the catacombs?
Impervious soldiers, trained with a download,

storming distant deserts or jungle against others
of their own kind, or even others of mine?
Underwater miners or void-bound farmers
unafflicted by a need to breathe, raising air-filled
domes to make more space for their makers?

Pitiful, beautiful slaves, bound
for existence (hardly a life)
without choice; no one should wish
to be one of you, no—but why then
do I feel such envy?

Bacchanal

he traded his robe for a lab coat
its filthy tail
sweeps through oil-sheened mud
flaps with back alley lurch
spine hunched in huddled conspiracy
hooves split bleeding
a black bile wine
reeled everywhere on the tainted ley lines
blind husk heeds
the zombie century call
hopes the fix fixes all
hops the walls
prints trickle behind
rolled up sleeves reveal
the needle
tracks of self consumption
sore of entry throbs
purple jellyfish
hissing mob slithers behind
hollow-eyed   supermodel squad
anexoria hot   pop singer dirty
wilted parrot plumage
used-up Maenads
hunting for another Orpheus
no talent required   any orifice will do
pop'n'play in the master bedroom
to the music artery beat   mad-eyed
waif kneels curls fragile fingers
in the wool of His hips
boy   girl   no matter
liberate the libation
gunshots outside   the undead
can't wait their turn
cultists sweating and trembling
in the Superdome

the worst of this generation
the best of this generation
bored to distraction
conjure Him   in the seedy glade
of tire ruts   beer cans   broken glass   hymens
clumsily torn
see the horns on his haggard head
glint in the headlights
of the pickup truck
sticks into snakes for everyone
curl them round your arm
to raise a vein
discover something new to do
for true   we're all born again
grown on our fathers' thighs
like a cancer

The Thirteenth Hell

Her voice in my ear said, *look, look.*
Though I squeezed my eyelids shut,
hid my face in my hands, I could still see it.

I pressed my fingernails in,
hooked my thumbs and pulled,
like so many here before. And
she said *look*, and I could still see it.

I crawled to the wall,
slammed my head on the stone,
found the cracks in the bone and clawed.
Her voice in my brain said, *look*,
and I could still see it.

I scrabbled at the ground
turned soft by my blood,
made a hole deep enough to force
my head in. She whispered from the earth,
look, look, and I could still see it.

The mud has swallowed me.
Things there feast on what's left
of what I used to be. And she
is one of them, her mouth moving
in my skull. *Look*, she breathes, *look*,
and I can still see it.

for Laird Barron

The Disturbing Muses

Nodding by night around my bed,
Mouthless, eyeless, with stitched bald head.
—Sylvia Plath

A. *canto d'amore*

Where did he find them, stone-gowned goddesses
who half a life later would bear
silent witness as their despairing disciple
swallowed poisoned air?

In the City of the Faceless he left them,
burned the maps that charted his return,
even burned those engraved on his skin.
He peeled their lacquer from his hand
that held the brush, nailed the bleeding glove
to a wall, beneath some blind and nameless
emperor's reproachful stare.

What she could not stop herself
from embracing,
he fled.
Behind him they tracked without eyes.
One howled
from the mouth that opened between its breasts
a word
shaped in the echo chamber of its heart
with no beginning or end.

B. *malinconia della partenza*

Amnesia through repetition:
that dour drooping face presided sadly
over copy after copy;
three dummy-headed dolls, their sorcery

badly diluted through decades
of insincere self-forgery.
His detractors said he whored his past for money.
He gladly let them believe it so.
Perhaps even he believed this so;
self-mocking at the end, passing off
bleak green skies as funny,
teasing artifice, a wry prank of the soul.

But six decades before
staring up at that sick twilight
he didn't find it funny at all.
Could he recall when it became
late afternoon forever,
when the long shadows froze?
Yes: the sick pain in his belly
still unsubsided, staring at the sculpture
of Dante in the Piazza Santa Croce
when the day itself coalesced
into marble and darkness.

Hours or days, he wandered:
the light never changed.
Moving enigmas, sails or trains
drifted soundless behind walls,
their cargoes hidden; he could not find
the other side, no more than he
could find a living soul.
                              Stumbling
among stark arcades, pale colonnades,
barren plazas, his survival
rested solely on an unseen denizen
who left food in incongruous places:
cluster of bananas beneath the aqueduct;
artichoke heads like war trophies
under the cannon barrel; pastries
found in places that defied the eye.

He thought, at one point, he had come
upon his savior: placed a hand on
the man's shoulder, turned him and

confronted blank mannequin face
with a single eye sketched
where brow should be.

Returned to bed, screaming,
believing he had seen the future.
The muses had made themselves known,
though he did not know it yet.
Still points of power,
triple nexus from which all stillness grew,
they awaited his arrival.

C. *archeologo*

Smokestacks stood watch on the horizon,
never breathing,
never close enough to touch.
Perspective was illusory
in this metaphysical space.
The profile of a face
seen outside the window
resolved itself as silhouette
of distant, impossible castle.

Still the food appeared.
Perhaps Ariadne herself—
her bare-breasted, resigned effigy
had so haunted him in Greece—
trying to lead him out of this time-twisted maze?
But every new exploration
brought him nearer to the heart, not away,
before the great red hand of the hour
swept him back.

Space made non sequitur:
Streets become walls,
tables become floors,
towers loom larger at distance
than up close. Here, entire ghettos
populated by crude mannequins;

there, mannequins as mountains,
bodies cobbled
from columned ruins.

Yet another empty piazza
beneath sinister green sky—
but what made these three blind muses
so magnify his unease?
Ruthless and primal,
stripped of all visage by the modern age.
One stood forever in shadow.
Did another shadow, smaller, dart behind?

No mouths with which to speak
but the silence itself chiseled words.

Bring us to her, it said.
Bring her to us.

A vision inside another's brain,
connected across the infinite,
transformed his own head.

D. *il sogno trasformato*

She found his painting somewhere humble,
a print in a book, stark black and white; and the same night
cowered beneath covers as three massive stone matriarchs
nodded above her knowingly. She dreamed
how their marble gowns enfolded her,
three mothers' overpowering embrace.

He knew

She dreamed her own face stitched shut,
skin tanned to leather thickness, implacable ovals
for mouth and eyes, rimmed with spiraling thread;
her slender form stiff as a tailor's dummy,
her blond tresses a wig anyone could remove and wear.

What hue

She dreamed herself again risen from ashes,
another failed attempt to do what she did best;
her red-haired vengeance, like Sisyphus' stone,
always rolling back on her. Flesh, bone,
but still nothing there.

He had painted

They kept eyeless vigil around her as she prepared;
their beautiful silence grew layered, an aching harmony
that approached the perfect stillness of immutable night.
They nodded approval as she stepped into their shadows,
turned the knob and opened the altar's door.

Her life, and despaired.
Now was the future, the future from which he fled,
          the future he fled into.

E. enigma dell'Oracolo

He painted, and copied, and copied,
and forgot the girl of his dreams.
Married a Russian immigrant after the wars,
her slender form still as a mannequin
as she posed for his brush,
her blond tresses ghostly on the canvas.

coda: mistero di una strada

At strange street's foot
a little girl in silhouette
runs with a hoop toward
a waiting shadow
which extends a stunted limb;
blacker and heavier than she,
it grows, as she ascends,
to meet her.

O'Keeffe's Bones

To me they are strangely more living
than the animals walking around . . .
They cut sharply to the center of something
keenly alive—vast, empty, untouchable—
that knows no kindness with its beauty.

No god could survive in the desert.
But dead gods
still can desire. Speak. Scheme.

They watched this small woman
with black hair pulled back taut,
her easels and determined paints,
her square face and gaze
deep as endless horizons.

They watched this small fierce woman
who did not know them, yet still she was drawn
away from the claustrophobic loveliness of Lake George,
from the claustrophobic darkness of New York,
from Alfred's claustrophobic love.

They spoke to her in subtleties.
In black rocks, beveled cliffs, bleached ivory.
They schemed in sand red as raw flesh.
Undaunted by the stark Catholic crosses
that captured her eye,
they chose their moment, and
she saw:

a head of blunt teeth, empty sockets, withered hide;
its jagged-bone grin dwarfed the Black Hills' wrinkled face,
its multitude of antlers curled
into the space above sky,
great branches of bone
which could hold moons as trees dangle fruit.

Sky gathered thunderheads in a mantle,
soaked the emptiness
beneath its rolling cloak,
spoke of beauty in fragments,
of love scoured clean of the mortal,
of the perfection of the faraway,
sad and majestic as skeletal landscapes
from which she never fully returned.

From her Ghost Ranch
she worshiped
and in the end worshiped alone,
her faith enough to flood a desert
with umber, to fill cracks in stone
with black rivers,

to saturate sands
with the cooling blues of night;
to give driest rock the vitality
of arterial blood.

Tanguy's Pebble

They thought de Chirico granted him the gift, and he
allowed everyone to believe, because the truth was far
too strange. He never shared it, not even with Kay,
until too late:

parted from his ship off the Argentine coast,
stolen by the sea gods, delivered, thirsty and freezing,
into the shadow of the Patagonian forest, where a serpent
like coils of fire punctured him in greeting; overhead

the arboreal sea rolled, as he crawled in delirium
over rocky mounds like glowing coral, slipped with a gasp
into sudden grottos, into a world of air like water, of wonders:

beings of plasma and stone; ribbons of curling intellect distilled
from form or purpose; entities of gem-hued mercury flowing
against each other in couplings of love or death; up or down

cast away like masts in a storm, no horizon, unbounded chasm,
warm gold-green stretching beyond sight; he swum, spun,
center of new cosmos, observer of infinities, himself observed—

a small thing, a pebble of liquid, no larger than a lima bean
drifted near, hovered at his fingertips like an inquisitive cat.
Anemone in miniature, his fingers closed—he felt little more
than a soap-bubble burst; fingers splayed again, the pebble gone.

All warmth extinguished. The universe, a roiling blue abyss.
Great hairy worm-things squealed, bleeding clouds of octopus ink.
Needle pyramids stabbed the void; wires like marionette strings
grew from nowhere, angled toward him, groped for his limbs.

He fled, in no direction and all, steered by fear beyond
    understanding,
to rouse, thrashing, in sheets soaked with ocean brine sweat; daylight

leaned in over the strange adobe arches of Rio Gallegos. Naked,
he stood before the mirror, a sea-hardened merchant mariner, Bible

perched by the basin like an accusation; stood, watched movement
beneath his skin, a throbbing lump the size of a pebble, submerged
into the meat below his wrist. No pain in his flesh, but an ache
that grew, a wanderlust no longer sated by waves against a hull

or foreign ports filled with women of exotic skins. His return
to Paris failed to ease that formless urge, till he read Breton,
felt hope stir. At first his efforts were crude, amateur-Dali,
but his pebbled hand, no matter how he fought, grew more sure,

opening windows to boundless regions he began to see
as home: underwater dreamscapes, crawling crystal cities,
peopled with animalcules of molten stone. He married troubled Kay,
herself adrift, who sensed how his soul trawled the deeps,

but couldn't share his mercurial bond, her paintings imperfect
refractions of that subtidal realm. Yet powers there sensed
their congregation of two, warned them of what leered from
over the Alsace; he saw it in the midst of a picnic, black cloud

hovering in the east, grinning, amoebic, exploded cubist skull—
or perhaps a different warning caused his westward flight.
Ensconced in America, he forced his dreams a different way,
exchanging water and crystal for desert and meshing line,

a new space where, perhaps, he hoped to slip away when
the marionette wires latched to him at last; resigned, homesick,
he put up no fight as they dragged him away, leaving poor Kay to
pore in confusion over the quicksilver pebble left behind,

that lodged in her arid dreams like the bullet
in her broken heart.

Picasso's Rapture

> Aphrodite is exacting a tribute of me for all my race.
> —Ovid, *Heroides*

1. *une femme*

There is no abstract art.
You must always start
with something. Afterwards
you can remove all traces of reality.

By the time of their meeting, he
was indeed a Master.
Removing her reality
took no more effort
than sketching a face on air.

The Minotaur's passion sated,
he left her a twisted, flattened shell,
curled like wet canvas on his padded chair,
mouth soundlessly screaming
from the same side of her face
that both eyes now started from.

He sighed in satisfaction,
then began the erasure.
Soon, no one there.
As with many before her.
He had not learned her name,
and did not care.

2. *son visage bleu*

Casagemas' head protruded
from the sheet that wrapped his

body; eyelids swollen,
temple stained black with
gunpowder, skin blue and
waxen in the candlelight.

Pablo watched them bear away
his best friend from Barcelona,
slain by a woman's refusal
as surely as she'd tugged his
fingers on the pistol with
puppet strings. Pablo knew
then: all women are witches.
Only an equal sorcerer
can survive them.

When the scarlet fever delirium
claimed him from Madrid,
he had lain in a down-stuffed bed
in a Catalonian mountain villa,
staring through a narrow window
at the verdant slopes; things seen
in that haze, shapes cavorting
in mid-air, opening doors
that weren't there, opening
space to show him views
from all angles at once.
Memories gnawed at the back
of his grieving brain: how to
find again that visionary state,
force it to obey his desires?

Until he found the first hints,
Casagemas' blue face swelled
behind every new encounter.

3. l'Arlequin

Some claim he infused those
thousands of canvasses with

hidden arcana, invocations
au culte mithraïque, tributes
to the god who slew
the celestial bull; had he heard,
Pablo would have laughed,
and rightly so, for the only alchemy
fused into his creations
was a magic he alone invented.

Against the skin of Fernande,
his first mistress, and first woman
he would claim to truly love,
the rapture of seeing outside
space returned, this time
to a clear, unfevered mind,
and he knew he could be
the new Harlequin, protégé
of trickster Hermes, author
of any wizardry his lusts demanded.

He painted himself,
handsome, sullen, clad in
diamonds of rose and black,
wearing Harlequin's peaked hat,
the nature of his magic
as yet unsculpted. He filled
the following years with a quest
for final configurations,
sharpened the vision that saw
from all sides at once, allowed
him to shape others to his whim.

And at last he shed
the Harlequin's chequered skin;
pierced and thrown away
with the toss of a horn
as he assumed the form
(distilled from the arenas
of Spain) that suited him best.

4. *Minotauromachia*

Do all women harbor a need
for annihilation? Most would deny it
but if one did yearn, he would find her,
smell her an auction hall away,
taste her scent amid hundreds
in the newly-opened gallery,
home in on her through
crowded streets; the Minotaur
weaving toward its meal.

As helpless as Europa draped
across the bull, she would come
to where he led, brook no struggle
as the Beast compressed,
flattened, conformed her
to its all-consuming vision.

Why not the genitals
in place of the eyes,
and the eyes between the legs?

Even those whom he allowed
names, whom he spared
the Bull's machinations:
what of them? One hanged,
two driven insane, one shooting
herself (just as Casagemas);
others that survived live on
only in the story he painted.

5. *son seul amour vrai*

How to reconcile the cocky hero
whose heart tore at the thought
of a Basque village bombed,
who painted a protest of

war's horrors, pressed postcards
of that protest into the hands
of Nazi soldiers, and yet
was never arrested; could the same
man be the Beast who tore
scores of women into surreal
contortions, and casually disposed
of the remains? Could one
divide himself so completely
into parallel planes?

Though he once imagined it so,
no avenging angel with hawk beak
and barrel chest ever descended
to stuff the Minotaur back
in its Harlequin cloak, bear
the wailing creature away.

Though he uttered the word
too many times to count,
only one woman truly earned
his adoration. As he lounged
in the Chateau Vauvenargue,
he recognized her form,
sensuous curves out of his
deepest dreams drawing into
focus. He readied himself
for the one mistress
that remained to conquer
or at last be bested by,
knowing he loved her truly,
knowing she loved him even more.

I think of Death all the time.
She is the only woman
who never leaves me.

new and uncollected poems

La Donna del Lago

For Claire Suzanne Elizabeth Cooney

Letter by letter, words trickled through the sand
blown before him on the shore by a wind
that bore the lake's own cool caress;
he failed to read them, eyes drawn skyward
by a lone black-winged speck that etched
lush loops beneath a canvas of clouds.

He came with easel, brush in hand,
himself not unlike a painting, skin
blended gesso pale, long black strokes
of hair. He propped up his own canvas,
paused, stood sculpture-still and marveled,
at a voice threaded through
the whistling breeze, the lapping waves.

Syllables not quite heard in full,
like fingers almost pressed along
the ridge of his cheekbone, against
the pulse beneath his chin, tilt his head,
aim his gaze at a column, a shimmer
above the water, a figure formed
of sunset light, of fleeting umbral fire,
and that molasses-sweet whisper flowed,
embedded in the shore's wet breathing.

He took a step, another, allowed
the lake to take soft hold of his ankles,
his knees, his thighs, as unnoticed
the black birds gathered above,
writing cursive lines on shifting slate.

Always, her voice, her silhouette of flame
ahead of him, as his feet left the shelf,
as his eyes lost the sky, as the drink
filled him in, as he drowned unknowing,
pursued her murmur down into the deeps.

Past the light's last grasp the space
opened into other realms—stars blinked
below him and swan-white maidens
swam among them, spread gossamer fins
to slip aside, circle him, pluck his clothes.
Their laughter brought no bubbles. Neither
did his protests as he sped his gait.

The fever he chased sported a face,
dark-eyed, a coaxing-ember smile
easier to see in the expanding dark,
receding as a comet races, over plains
of magma murk where spined and shelled
imps bent to their work, harvested
the hollow-eyed dead for cooking pots
and tentpole torture games. They waved
their claws his way but he kept on,
his tapered sylvan feet well out of reach.

In a luminous demesne he at last became
entangled, nearly severed from his star
amidst a tightening lattice of hungry
radiance that craved all his layers
and would not be denied, until black forms
sliced their cursive from below, freed him
from the listless weight of flesh,
filled his arms with hues and shadows,
and lines to sew them in a greeting gift.

He stood before her, naked, reed-slender, blue
as the current that claimed him, black hair
in a cirrus crown, and dared to encroach
upon the corona draped over her shoulders,
the mist cinched at her waist, the aurora
of her tresses, to lay the circlet woven
of his soul's final art upon her brow.
And her speech came clear,
her syllables embraced.

Washed up on the rocks, his body
showed no wear, his dreamy smile
translucent as a half-remembered sunset.

Carrington's Ferry

What threat
could these scaly oarsmen ever pose?
She dodged Miró's famished halo
of animalcules, Picasso's rutting minotaur,
Tanguy's liquid, probing pebbles.
Deflected Dali's softening emissions.
Sidestepped Duchamp's fractured descent.
Her Cerberus grew far more heads
than most. She kept the one whose kiss
she chose to return, and killed
any others who rashly fought off sleep.
Compared to them, this boatful of lizards,
this hooded ferryman with forked tongue
has no hope in hell of harming her.

She looks back
at the red-gowned women,
the graceful petals of their heads,
pale orchid blooms, nodding
with the rhythm of the wind.
Will they warn her
if her next step goes awry?

She'd first glimpsed them in the English gardens
where she frolicked as a girl, but
they never spoke, offered no chat,
unlike the slow, thoughtful statues
or the stained glass peacocks who
would happily shriek her ears off—
Don't let them send you away, they pleaded,
Come back to us, come back to us.

How she tried, rebelled against her schoolmasters
whether at work or play, kept her attention
focused in other space, the space she meant to see.

How tight the sheets they wrapped her in
to trap her, drag her silent from the hedgerow maze.
No matter how shallow her footprints,
the thunderous black beast sniffed out her path,
the stone of her father's face crowning its shoulders,
battlements shielding his ears, eyes empty
as her hopes of escape. She would be a gift
to the King, a dainty mosaic mortared
in his courtyard, a bauble of fancied flesh.
She attempted epic quests, all the time
the tether-thread coiled around her wrist,
drawing her back to the drawing room.

Until the orchid maids nodded.

The tunnel to their altar opened in his chest,
this silver-haired, sly-smiling German,
rimmed with light, shaded with night,
the passage opening and opening into his
body and beyond, her thread redirected inside,
a guide to navigate a new labyrinth—
she left a chortling hyena in her ballroom clothes
and stole off to Paris, walked naked
past the all-consuming artists' eyes
and told that dirty Spaniard Miró
to fetch his own damn cigarettes.
Her Max, already wed; but he could not
and would not deny her.

And the demons
climbed from blood-soaked soil,
too many to resist, and pried him away;
laughing through dog fangs,
kicking with jackboots,
snarling with panther muzzles,
armored with Panzer hide,
running her down as she fled,
carrying her into the Spanish asylum
where they pinned her down and
racked her with volts, poisoned her brain,
ground against her bucking spirit,

quested to invade the maze, hunting
for the gate she desperately held shut.
Her father sent a rescuer by submarine
but as the taxi rushed the Lisbon street
a voice heard from the wrong end
of a trumpet whispered new instructions
and she demanded instead the embassy
to Mexico—what chance Picasso's
startled friend would greet her there?
What chance, in the distance past his shoulder,
she'd see pale orchids nod their stately heads?

The Nazis could not reach her anymore,
nor the *nouveau riche* or the House of Lords.
The hero twins called on her, the hunter
and the jaguar, the grinning monkeys
and the serpent who gifted her
with feathers of every color,
fierce Frida and her monster Diego.
If she ever grew weary from their company,
she could always steal into the hedgerows,
her private garden where mannered harpies
poured tea and priestesses bowed their horns,
attendants in crow masks bathed exquisite vultures
and butterfly-winged sphinxes guarded their eggs
as Tarot trumps walked arm in arm,
witchey trinities mixed spells in flower cups
and faces peered from canopies,
playful ghosts snagged in the trees.
Asked where she birthed the wonders,
she snapped, *You overthink. It's about
seeing, about visions into other space.*
Both lands loved her in return.
For decades she dreamed, long since freed
of any limits.

Stone touched by her fingertips took flight.

* * *

In the maze, dark waters rise.
The orchid maids watch.
The ferrymen wait.
She snorts at them and turns
the other way.

She walks across the forest, looming
into the sky. The wheat stalks
of her hair channel the sun.
She unfastens her robes, exposes
hieroglyphs etched on her skin.
Birds spill from beneath her breasts,
shade the countryside with outstretched wings.

Machine Guns Loaded
with Pomegranate Seeds

A thousand Persephones lie bleeding in the Lethe,
a thousand more cross on Charon's armada,
proud brows gleaming, hair windswept,
the first shawls they made once they taught themselves to knit
clutched to their shoulders, flak-jacket secure.
Behind the sandbags crouch the grunts of Hades, primed to feed
a thousand chains of regret through greasy barrels.
We peer through sniper slots
at the enemy's gowned grace,
shudder, rub our hands, wish for breath
to warm our palms, wait sadly for the order
to serve the feast.

Ascending

For Tom Disch

The escalator, rolling ever down,
has reached an end at last and here you lie
as lonely as a sailor left to drown—
like your trapped hero, we cannot know why.

The roaches march in lockstep to commands
like convicts programmed for unwelcome war,
a war that's lost though no one understands
but you, who tried to warn us once before

what lies in wait for red-faced arrogance.
"We are all cripples"—you, alone, divine,
a smirking Momus whose knife-twirling prance
drew blood to fill our cups of dream-dark wine.

Your Resurrection surely won't take long:
your demon words borne high on wings of song.

Sisyphus Crawls

Sisyphus crawls
toward the honeydew-sweet air,
toward shadows of clouds beneath the bright skies' undersphere,
and the hornets storm the towers of his head,
the windows of his eyes cave in,
the friezes etched beneath the dome of skull
crumble down his throat,
faces broken away.

Sisyphus crawls
toward leaves like soft sylph wings,
toward the poetry of bird and wind,
and his atmosphere becomes thick as water,
dense as deep abyss descent,
and his arms snap from the pressure,
fold in upon themselves and tear away,
spine splinters, ribs cleave in,
broken buttresses beneath
a violated undersea dome.

Sisyphus slithers
toward new rain like soft cool hands,
toward the chatter in shaded streets,
toward the rumpled warmth of home,
and the passage compresses
like gravity, like singularity,
twists him into pieces cell from cell,
stripped, flayed, pared
into coils of seared mourning,
trickle-streams of silent wail,
into weeping ash,
into less, and even less,
and smaller still.

And these motes,
flushed past all light,
begin their slow climb anew,
their rise toward reunion,
the underworld's laughingstock,
its phoenix toy, bonded
by the cruelest joke of all,
the single thought that never breaks its hold:
The gate never closes.
The gate never closes.
The gate is never closed.

The King of Cats, the Queen of Wolves

WITH NICOLE KORNHER-STACE AND SONYA TAAFFE

1.

These gouges where glaciers furrowed toward the sea
were smooth-sloped still, ice-muscled, snowbound;
these waves, a salt-waste of frozen crests: and we
were handprints of smoke on ochre walls, the ghosts
of birds in dying flutes, the first time (they say)
the king of cats and the queen of wolves clashed.

Time had no current, lay still in all directions.
Gods and beasts and beast-gods stalked
each other across star-hot sand, through
tree-high grass, into forests that swathed
continents, where dragons long as rivers
shimmered through the branches, beneath
nights deep as the teeming abyss of Sea.
He walked alone across tundra oceans,
danced deadly through infinite verdant canopies;
she ghosted the ground beneath, golden eyes
seeking from shadow, a glint of silver and sable
in primeval snow. Her children huddled always
beneath her cloak, still without voice or form;
he had no followers, but the strength of a host.

Charcoal crumbled across a cavern's ribs. Limestone
stained with torchlight, smoothed with time. Here
his eyes glint blackly, and there her tracks mark
north, truer than iron; but meteors fell and blazed
like untold angels as her teeth raked his throat,
his claws set in her shoulders, and here red ochre
smears for their blood that glittered (they say)
into garnet where it fell. How she tore her mouth
free to scream down the moon, how the tides
bulged and spilled over at her tempestuous howl;

how his strength rippled as he dragged the earth
aside, one hooked and contemptuous shrug,
and the delta lay differently then. Ice-floes
into warm swamps, magma cracking upward
beneath chill plains, sand skidded into snow
and all the globe torn awry in their battle:
all the nameless powers of beforetime rapt
to see whose children would inherit the earth.

Salt of blood and salt of ocean were one,
libations of violence that drenched day into night.
The might of their convulsions subsided, as must
all aftershocks; the outcome of their intimate war
undecided: each had torn the other countless ways,
subdivided selves roaming broken terrains, tundras
wrenched from jungles, peaks ripped from plains.
The battle neither won nor lost: momentum fractalled
in infinite directions, unfocused by entropy;
only the children, single cells of once great gods
remained, things of claws, teeth, stalking, silence,
united in death and hunger and hatred.

Time, punctured in fury, began its flow.

2.

The hall bustles with finery; to gaze
upon such silk and lace, white fur and blood-
red sashes, ribbons twined in wigs, a dance
of noble plumage, is to know that time
is just a toy to each pale-powdered face,
a strange place to resume epochs-old hunt;

yet silent blows the horn that starts the hunt
when, stepping to the flute, her wary gaze,
so vulpine-sharp, alights upon his face,
its supple bones, a smile that could draw blood;
a raging echo from the birth of time
commands them both, and as they close to dance,

their spirits have entwined unseen and dance
quite differently through half-remembered hunt,
claws and teeth that tore at flesh and time
a whirlwind through their minds as they gaze
into each other's eyes, a taste of blood
tinting both their tongues as they face

each well-remembered, unfamiliar face
that paces in this politesse. This dance
traced to a pattern deeper still than blood
or bone that yet might falter in the hunt—
if minuets have tamed her moon-burned gaze
to shadowplay, worn token over time,

or if, within this masquerade of time,
he has misplaced his lover's, killer's face—
but watch how sleekly he bows to her gaze
and how her fingers vise his in the dance
as though his skin might slip. Now for the hunt
that reckons its spoils in more ways than blood;

a breath passed back and forth, the beat of blood
that faster than their measured steps keeps time
to the race of hearts, tuned to her hunter's
silence mirrored in his lean-eyed face
as finally he pulls her close to dance
beneath the hall's incurious, ageless gaze.

Her lip-rouge stained like blood upon his face,
where for a time he trapped her in his dance—
the hunt releases them to their shared gaze.

Perhaps in an unfathomable design
woven tight as atoms, deeper than sea,
fabric firmed before ruptured time's flow,
all odds of enmity require this chance:
two things born from hate will meet and love,
and spin the clay of fear into new shapes.

In the dark their shadows form one shape,
that etches strange calligraphy, a sign
announcing the unknown, new forms of love
born in a humble chamber; do they see,
the courtesans dancing below? What chance
have they to sense the tremors flow

through time's thin web, as lovers flow
against each other, pressing savage shapes
onto startled skin; without a chance
to understand the shiver in the air, this sign
of shattering change, the heedless dancers see
to their steps with masked facades of love

pressed cheek to cheek; how we all love
to hook limbs in bestial pairings and flow
in practiced mimicry of rites born in the sea
and before, when a mate or killer took shape
in the dark and a partner awaited the sign
to join or flee. As below, so above, a chance

meeting of godsparks leaves the world no chance
to spin unchanged; their furor masked as love
bent on mutual destructions, all the signs
clawed in their skin, in teeth marks that flow,
in the taste of each other's blood, shapes
their bodies form, echoes of that struggle seen

before time began. At the height do they see
these fragments embedded within? Is there chance
for them to glimpse these primal shapes,
the Queen astonished in the power of her love's
embrace, the startled King's arch and flow—
Fate's tapestry restitched in new design.

Seeking meaning in this unexpected love,
at first chance she asks scrying water's flow
what shape the child will take, but gleans no sign.

3.

From the pierced heart of the world, time gouts
and stutters, gouts and trickles to surcease. The hall
is wrack, cold carrion beneath a sunless noon, spoils
of no war but entropy. So too the other battlefields
and bridebeds have flared and dimmed, each one a pan-flash
in a plate of ice, each imprinted with its sullen,
crimson ghost. She stalks what once were roads. Moons
pare themselves to nothing and ripen anew, rearing
through a pall of ash; neither her cat's eyes nor
her wolf's nose deign to crave that feeble light. She walks:
as one, the ghosts of ghosts, pale hunting-trophies
on time's bloodied belt, will turn to her, then cringe away—
and each one wears her face. At her footfall, holographic flowers
    flicker out.

It was not always thus. Her hunt was once a hunt; the city once
a city, or a ruined city, or a meadow where a ruined city stood.
Now there are walls, or ghosts of walls, or ivy clutched
to nothing where the ghosts of walls once loomed: no fire
rains down around her; no wolf's-claw, cat's-claw banners raised
where she had thought to sleep (though their holograms, archived
in the city's histories, do flicker in and out betimes, in quick
succession, or else overlaid, one veining through the other like
a leaf held to the sun). Her mother's bloodline
and her father's both reach back and back through time, hand over
hand, as though drawing pails up from dry wells—but never
forward, and none remain to tell her her own secrets. She camps
the murals 'til they round their circuit, flicker in: she sees the cities
rise, the feline and the lupine both; she sees the walls forget
who raised them; she sees each one's inhabitants go interloping
through the other's gates; she sees wars, détentes, truces
sublimated into legend as the bombs wail down—truces forged anew
upon the finding of a common enemy: the spreading web of by-
    blows
with hearts that pump the blood of both. Now they are dust, her
    mother's
kin, her father's; she alone slogs on, despite their greatest efforts
unannihilated, though the shots still dog her dreams, and she wakes

ducking, rolling, baring claws her grandam's grandam might
have worn, which every time resolve to fingertips, soft and unavailing,
in the light.

They say (they *said*, for who remains to say?)
the king of cats, the queen of wolves died childless,
were each reborn, and childless died again: each iteration torn
from his/her father's/mother's side, a tumor whose metastasis
gnawed worlds to dust, sucked stars like eggs, raked time's weft
shrieking out of true. Thronged by ghosts of her past selves she hunts,
each feinting as she feints, each pouncing at the shadow of the
        one before,
each emptyhanded, emptyclawed, clean-toothed and parched
for blood. By her cat's-heart's, wolf's-heart's metronome she walks,
the last in line, the shadowless, unmoored in time, and trusting to
her mother's strength, her father's luck: when at last a shadow
turns to her unbidden, eyes glazed with lust for blood or flesh,
her muscle memory will give reply; when at last time wakes from
        stasis,
shakes her clinging from its crippled back, regardless for how long,
how far she falls, she will land always, always
on her feet.

The Parcae

Three dark sisters speak to me
through doors that stand ajar
beneath the veined dome,
this ivory Pantheon circling the bed
where I lie but never sleep.
They speak from adjacent rooms
so distant they could be portholes
to other worlds, their voices
a soft, constant susurrus.

Perhaps some century past
I screamed for them to let me be,
told them the sounds they make
affect me like the spider's prickle
on the skin in the moment
before dreaming, jab slumbers
away like sweet fruits pulled ever
out of reach. Perhaps in some
unremembered past I've begged
them for peace, but now I hold
my tongue for fear they would
obey, withdraw, leave nothing
but the light they block as my
sleepless hours stretched on
and on and on in utter silence.

One sister tells me she's a healer,
one who prolongs the living and eases
the passage of the dead; she stands
in the crack, tall as a grandfather clock
and gaunt, every rib etched by shadow,
teeth long and yellow as she promises
elixirs brewed to still me inside.

One sister tells me she's a scholar,
that the dark fluids staining her skin
black in the moonlight are the inks
spilled in her studies, that the smell
wafting from her is binding glue gone soft
after countless times she's cracked
those ancient spines. She pleads
to read to me, lips against my ear,
sink me in her timeless tar of words.

One sister tells me she's a warrior,
her arm extended through the gap
to wave not her open hand but an
open blade. With eye fixed on me
tiger-fierce she tells me she offers
no lie, only the simplest solution.

They urge, choose, choose, and they
will wait until I do, until I call,
and then maybe one, maybe all those
doors will creak wide, a bright final
agony before all light mutes and hushes
—and I let them wait. Their voices
hiss with addictive poison, cajole,
caress; scrape, prick, draw blood,
numb and then shake me, startle me
alive, and only to their music can
my self-deluded soul pretend to dream.

To Sail the Leaden Sky

Where have all the madmen gone?
The ones who ordered their names inscribed
along the flanks of their rocketships
in letters of solid gold six feet high?

The boys who tuned their radios
to catch broadcasts from other timestreams,
built capsules in their basements
that flipped gravity upside-down?

Did all their riches and transistors
fail to bridge Einstein's distance?
Did they quake at quantum leaps?
Shrink from the lush curls of superstrings?

Now they wait in deep bunkers
hoarding vacuum tubes and magnets,
mushrooms bathed in cathode light,
bulky helmets strapped on in hopes

the perfect lightning strike
bestows the right frequency of ESP,
the one that lets them reverse the polarities
and will the world flat once more.

The Problem with Science Fiction Poetry

Science fiction poetry sings castrati songs,
whines wistfully for stars and princesses fair
but cowers from stalking unexplored plateaus,
tearing alien throats and eating unknown flesh,
losing its chance to fuck like mad and leave
crying children in the nooks of every timeline.
It shrinks from breaking open young worlds
and reading the molten innards; cringes
from forcing you inside the museum case,
crammed hard against the dying and exotic;
choosing instead to find ever cuter ways
to rewrap your worn-out childhood toys.

Kandinsky's Galaxy

Color provokes a psychic vibration.
Color hides a power still unknown
but real, which acts on every part
of the human body.

The spiral circumscribes a center, but no limits.
Nothing held there and
nothing there that desired to be held.
The populace falls up,
shedding confinements of skin and shadow,
riding the inverse surge of gravity
as light and line.
To yearn for flight
is to fall into forever,
every landing a new abyss.

Before his century arrived
he abandoned numbers for art,
abandoned a wife for a mistress,
abandoned a mistress for a wife,
till he at last found a companion
who could withstand deepest space.

The more frightening the world becomes
the more art becomes abstract.

He refused the most sure sanctuary,
hands extended, again and again,
promising escape to America.
He brushed them all away,
not trusting the beautiful void
to seek him out once more if he fled.

A human telescope aimed
at an angle no other could perceive,

focus adjusting over decades,
foregrounded first in the fey realms,
noting the tiny stars that crawled
through river flows
and couples in love.
Yet these lights shone from nowhere close.
The vast distance apparent
as he bent his lens.

His gaze rose through the shapes
behind the world,
the aggressive disputes
between entities without boundaries,
fields of mud and blood and blue
warring on the skins
of creatures without faces
seen in perilous closeup.
For so many years
those hostile clouds blocked his view.

Yet he had to strain further,
never dared stray too far
from his vantage—even
when the Bolsheviks took his home,
when the Nazis shut his school,
he only ran as far as Paris
and stayed put when the Nazis joined him.
The calming void
came to him each time he closed his eyes.

Those stars were letters swimming at creation's edge,
glyphs larger than galaxies,
moving over and under and around one another,
an endless ever-changing text,
new epics written with each shift in space.
He strove to read them,
captured in frustration on his canvas
mere words, snatches of calligraphy,
fragments of a cosmic alphabet.

When his own colors began to fade,
huddled by the wood stove,
hands afire with a vision of two great towers,
posts for a gateway to emptiness policed by ghosts,
he recognized he might, before his soul
broadcast out into the dark,
transcribe a single sentence.
It would have to be enough.

Perhaps the letters aren't in proper order.
Perhaps no one born since
could piece the map together,
place galaxies true in their quadrants,
connect the constellations.
But walk the ascending spiral.
Storms of shape and hue rain tremors
somewhere parsecs deep behind your eyes,
yet still electric, urgent,
spurring you to climb,
to slice through the harness of gravity
and fall into the codex written
at the boundary of time.

Color is the key. The eye is the hammer.
The soul is the piano with its many chords.
The artist is the hand that sets
the soul to vibrating.

Deluge

"Every time you take a drink of water, you're
drinking recycled star material. Our bodies are
created entirely of star stuff."
—*National Geographic*

When he learned he could drink the stars, he vowed
that even one burning sphere could never be enough
to quench the thirst that ached in all his shriveled cells;
he longed to pour galaxies down his throat, consume
cold dwarfs and exploding novas, suck cotton candy
nebulae through his teeth, chew the baby stars
inside like sunflower seeds, wolf dark matter gulfs
in gassy gulps and mow through Andromeda spirals
like a starved teen through meatlover's pizza. He longed
to turn himself inside out. Envelop and swallow
the universe. Stuff his stomach on bloated creation.
Spill acid back to the Big Bang. Show God
how real cleansing gets done, primordial soup
breakdown way more wicked than Noah's flood.

TimeFlood

WITH IAN WATSON

Why did they dam the river of time some way upstream?
How did they dam time itself? Maybe they fought—will fight—
a probability war, striving to block some streams of possibility
and reinforce others. A myriad dams might be made. Sabotage
may ensue, and rival dams, to divert events a different way.

The result is that time flooded backward catastrophically,
causing such eddies and whirlpools and deeps and shallows.
A billion people lived their whole lives in mere seconds
and expired in ignorance. Others were flotsam on the flood,
seeing cities and civilizations rise and fall around them.

Caught up in an eddy, a mother-to-be found herself
kneeling at the grave of her greatgranddaughter. Stretched
by the current, a soldier shot dead in a two-minute war
suckled for centuries at his mother's tit. By the time he hit
the ground a glacier was engulfing the battlefield.

And me? And me? She grew instantly old
in my shrinking arms as I became a child again,
held tight by a blind crone. I lead her along
by her wrinkled hand, my grandmother so it seems,
who still whispers endearments toothlessly

as we make our way though the ruins of millennia,
wrecked rude huts, tumbled temples of marble,
fallen castles, twisted girders of skyscrapers,
and so much mud where at least food grows,
in search of an Eden from where time may have sprung,

a fountain of youth to restore to her some
of my unwanted juvenility. But this Earth
of multiple eras is vast, survivors are few
and mostly insane, and yesterday for the first time
I saw, to my horror, the corpse of a dinosaur.

Seed the Earth, Burn the Sky

The mountain god wakes,
stretches out his arms, laughs
a laugh to burn the timid moon,
and I explore the crags
of his torso with my hands,
trace the runnels of his belly,
the clefts of his chest,
the vales of his hips,
the secret, sacred pools boiling below.

The mountain god takes
my head in his hands, plunges
me in fire, holds me under till I melt,
crushes me into new shapes and
drags me up again,
and whatever form he molds me in
I dance
I dance as candleflame
I dance against his fingers
I dance to torch the pits of his eyes
I dance as he cremates me again

The mountain god scrapes
the sky with his wings, arches his neck,
bellows his echoes to me,
and every pale ghost I have ever held inside
swarms out, fountains up,
shades of baying beasts, of bone mutations
sacrificed to him in helpless cascade,
in a gale that shreds the air, howling as it rises
to rain upon the heavens,
to seed the sky.

The mountain god folds
(The morning bell sounds)

himself into the earth,
(The mourning bell tolls)
softens into loam,
(The morning bell accuses)
and I inhale his mud,
(The bell extols the end)
let him smother me beneath.
(of night, of breath, of spirit)
The day will never have me.

Surviving Wonderland

"I am the White Rabbit,"
says the creature in the mirror
that's neither rabbit nor white.
It speaks with a boy's voice
behind its loose-skin mask,
but you see no lips moving,
only a black-greased gear
turning amidst hoses
that pulse, misplaced trachea.
It raises claws to the glass,
clicks them on the silver side.
"I shall be late," it says.
"So very late."

Over its seething shoulder,
across from you in Wonderland,
an empty pinafore mimics
your nervous pose. Jointed pipes
slide out from beneath its hems,
tentacles from an anemone,
retract in again. "Don't look,"
the rabbit-not-a-rabbit-says.
"Don't look at her. The new Queen
claimed her head, and most
of the rest." Nails click the glass.
"Open this. Open this."

Wheeled into view
from outside the mirror frame,
a small form squirms in a crib,
except the bed is a flower,
the bars are Venus flytrap teeth
fighting to close, to squeeze
the life it holds into submission.
Rabbit Mask follows your gaze.

"Do you fear for it? Don't.
It's not a child, it's a beast.
If you help me open this,"
clickety-clack, "You'll see
I'm telling you the truth."

Alice never held a weapon.
She obeyed treacherous signs,
infiltrated deep, seized her moment,
smashed the house of cards,
grabbed the monarchs, shook them
into different shapes. So what
is that object gleaming
in your grip, fingers coiled,
knuckles pressed pale
around its steel handle?
To get what you want,
you risk opening the nest.
"Yes," it says, clack-click,
"I'll arrive right on the dot. Just
bring that hammer down. Please,
bring that hammer down."

The Duelists

You'll know them by their asymmetries.
Their iron limps, their sleeves loose over
missing limbs, their patches, their veils,
their masks. They clomp the cobbles,

scrape bricks with their hooks, click
rhythms beneath their coats with blades
long as canes. Their bloodstains blotch
the streets. There, another contest begun,

wooden teeth clenched in concentration.
One saws above the elbow of his own
already truncated arm, the other, not
to be outdone, hacks at a leg, striking

his shin with splintering blows. Whoever
can lose the most and live will win
the row. They say demons with white hot
scales consume them from inside, else

how to explain the urge to accede
to that first dare, to whittle off skin,
snip fingers, crush molars, slice away
what's held beneath the tourniquet,

glorying in what's shed or weeping
when they've failed to shed enough.

The Vigil

for Nicole Kornher-Stace

She waits atop the lacerated hill—
with crags stretched from its slopes like pleading hands—
astride a mare of straw and bark and bone
with witchfire embers burning in its heart,
as she surveys the cobalt lands below,
an ever-shifting plain of weeping smoke.

Where her eyes affix cannot be guessed.
Beneath a hat of iron wire
hang tattooed skins that veil her face.
The rifle resting on her thigh
shines silver even without moon or sun,
against a long skirt sumi black.
The bandoleers crossing her breasts
are lined with teeth, her collar's lace
spun from skeins of blood.
The claws of scarabs hold her hems in place.
The membranes of her veil twitch with her breath.

The coils of smog below sometimes part
to grant coy glimpses of the hoi polloi,
their flesh gone grey, their springs torn loose,
their gears gutted, throats mauled.
Those unharmed by other plagues lie sprawled
where they were shot. No arms lift,
no lips whisper, no legs stir.

If something starts in motion,
so will she:
Her steed combust and roar to life,
her veil pulse,
her weapon howl.
If even a soul stirs,
so will she.

127

The Black Watch

The Black Watch ghosts between the hills
on silent horses whose hooves
stir no dust on the bone-dry road.

Beneath their thatched roofs villagers cower,
wrap themselves in their own shadows;
rub ash in their eyes to hide the tell-tale shine

as they shudder under beds of straw.
Young mothers clutch their newborns close:
a babe who can't be silent may be silenced.

Those still cursed with scraps of Talent
cut their childrens' fingertips
and draw blooded sigils above their doors;

beg friendly demons to fade their homes
into the dark, whisper unwanteds away.
But somewhere, the Watch will knock.
The door unlock, creak wide.

Which home will give shelter
to the Black Watch on this night?
Whose house hold a smiling family
of bones come morning?

Unland, Unlife

WITH ANITA ALLEN

They've never found the bodies out at sea
but every day they wash up on our shore,
dressed in shirts and shifts or even gowns,
both hands, left feet punched through with
wounds that never heal or bleed.

Left untouched in the water, they'll wake up,
walk inland, build lives, towns, even ships
for hunting answers on a sea that never yields.
For when these immigrants ask where, how, why,
we shrug and rub our own bloodless stigmata.

Reynard the Revenant

See this bone that's clenched between my jaws,
this snout too slight for breaking ribs like bread?
Wicked sparks like stardust from my claws.

Why did the Sentries raise no warning caws,
shrill birds who surely spied my four-toed tread?
Who crunched those bones so fine in narrow jaws?

At my wake rough beasts faked tears of loss.
My corpse-ears pricked up in my wooden bed.
Evil mists like stardust from my paws.

The greedy Wolf howled till a sudden pause,
faced by a foe too clever to stay dead.
Now here's a skull, clenched silent in my jaws.

Only slysters rewrite cosmic laws.
The Lion's pelt slumps over fur slicked red.
Evil drips like king's blood from my claws.

Hear the hounds bay mourning for their boss—
the hunter's lost his antlers. And his head.
See these savory bones crunch in my jaws.
Wicked shines like stardust in my paws.

skíouroi moirōn

Hear: the motion in the trees,
patter-patter in the hollow trunks,
crawling, crawling, crawling down
to the grottos where winds howl through roots

See: the grey forms swarm
down those roots that arch like ribs,
ribs that hold the world's skin
stretched taught above this measureless den
where the gods echo, invisible

Feel: the grey forms flowing down—
small eyes glint, small hands scrabble
at the edge of this pit where you've lain
so long hoping for rescue, so long
hoping to see a friendly face
peer over the lip. Not
long paired teeth, flared fur tails,
so many the walls seethe

Hear: the grotto sing back your screams,
sing them out through the hollows of the trees
as the gods feed

Hungry Constellations

Prologue: Possibilities

Like the giants who boil under the land,
whose broken baby teeth form mountains,
or their sisters who seethe unbearable heat
in crevasses beneath the sea,
stars burn with appetite,
huge and slow,
diffused and directed through the legends
that pin them in place.

Another cosmos, a mere crêpe layer away,
shall afford us the best seats in the house.
Peel aside the sweet starch of time and distance
and step through. Here
the night sky's the stage once
the curtain of day rises.
Celestial bodies array themselves at impossible speeds,
acting out their stories in real-time for a globe-spanning audience.

The peoples here watch from their chateau skylights,
from their glassine-flimsy city domes,
from broad ships like wooden continents,
from arid plain and barren rock and glacier palaces.
Even the fey, real as you or I,
herd their captives out to catch the show,
the scattered soup of night become platform and proscenium.

How these incendiary orbs
hunger for our observation, our admiration,
the power of the human eye to enliven what's devoid.
With ardor they devour the scripts we dream for them,
then improvise.

Constellations shift before our eyes,
their tales our tides.
Their shadows our losses.
Their orbits our lies.

The Fox Smiled, Famished

Gather around.

Gather around the largest fire of all,
large enough to warm the lands
on the other side of the world,
to brighten all your moons.

My burning coat swells redder by the day.
My teeth are curls of flame, my tail a flare.
My tale? Come closer. Hear it.
Closer still—the ending is a secret.
Each of you will hear
as I whisper in your ear.
Other planets joined this circle before yours, yes.
I cannot fathom where they've gone.
Come closer yet and I'll share my guess.
You're practically standing on my nose,
basking in my boiling breath.

Let me pick you up, little world,
little pup in my jaws.

The Serpent Is Tempted

It's a principle of the universe
that everything spirals
to an intimate squeeze—
the sinuous limbs of galaxies,
the crush of gravity.

I have no fruits for you to pluck—
they shine so far away, so hot,
how could you reach?
How could you bite?—
it's *your* hidden warmth,
your blood-salt oceans,
the scattered lights of your
night-time habitats like
so many wide-eyed mice,
that call to *me*.

Dim stars demarcate my spine,
winding side to side
as I slide to you.

How I long
to flicker subtleties
before your eyes,
twin comet tails
joined in a forked tongue.
How I long
to thaw
against your molten heart.

The Spider Sends Gifts

The event horizon
bounds the edge of my web.
Your scholars claim nothing can emerge from my silk,
no morsels that alight within, not even
my own burnt-cinder body.
Shine the spotlight here, you'll see nothing,
maddening absence,
and even more troubling hints of motion
as the sleek, dark arches of my legs
quiver at frequencies undetectable
by eye alone.

Then,
the milkweed spill scatters from my funnel,
wriggling specks of stardust drifting,
spinning light,
Doppler strands lengthening behind,
firework sparks burning brighter as they
crawl to you—
all my hundred thousand babies,
hunting for new homes.

The Crow Migrates from the Outer Dark

Alone among the cosmic menagerie, I am defined
not by bones drawn in stars but by black between;
as my wings eclipse, their desperate shine
bends around my feathertips, begging for your gaze.

To you, lovely worms, I'm but a lone eye
staring back at you on deepest nights
when your fires gutter out and the turbines
that charge your cities falter.

So far away you still haven't noticed
how each year my single star glows brighter,
plunging inward at the speed of light.

The curve of my wings once marked
the rim of the universe.
They still do,
that boundary shrinking
with my eons-long dive.

When I arrive, your sons and daughters
countless generations hence—those who survived
the fox's snapping jest, the thousand spider nests,
the serpent's airless smother—will see naught
in their sky but the emptiness inked in my quills,
the scavenging void's sharp beak.

Interlude: Truth

The truth, some claim, has a portrait of its own
riddled through the Cosmic Sphere's black shell
that admits its deep blue light,
refraction of an unseen power.

The fey pestilence who in this layer of what can be
hold sway in forest mounds and mountain hearts
claim these pinpricks of azure
are not stars, but tunnels outside time,
the heads of the trails they followed, that ended here.

Yet what shape do these mysteries take in this sky?
Some claim a lyre, longing for fingers
to coax songs of grief and war.
Some claim a balance, its empty scale
fed human hearts found wanting.
Some claim a veil, which hides a face
that aches for our regard, its beauty
sure to blind all beholders.

The Hunter Takes Aim

So many villains fill this sphere with their lanterns.
My own stars dance to sketch a bow, draw back
to manifest an arrow.

The boys among you cheer
to see me rise broad-shouldered,
my breastplate stained with pale blood of nebulae,
my belt clustered with glowing hides.

The wise among you wonder
whose skins hang flayed
when predatory stares populate the sky
from horizon to zenith.
Do they dare wonder aloud?

In your lands squat my temples
of marble and topaz, almost beautiful
as the square-jawed, cleft-chinned,
sharp-cheekboned face
enshrined within—
the effigy you've masked me in,
exquisite and unblinking.
Millions kneel before my gaze
and avert their eyes.

No wastelands more hostile exist
than the surfaces of stars and
the gulfs they sail.
Question what allegiances I've made to survive
and my faithful will find you,
their aim as sure as mine.

The Prince Tightens His Embrace

My jeweled arms join, a glittering circle.
All that's wed to me sealed between them.
All you will bear for me stays crushed
close to my heart. I force your orbits
smaller and smaller. My fury grows
each time you try to move. When I die of rage
the burst will tear you atom from atom.

The Dragon Shields Her Young

I am

a river of stars and scales and fire and milk and all the things that
thrive in the alchemical reactions where they meet.

I am

my own soul and all the others too, every single constellation in the
sky. Not one of them can stop the chimerical redactions as I claim

their shapes, their minds. I do this at will, but they can never in return claim mine.

The gale of my flight strips the fox's fiery hide. My coils ensnare the serpent, braid him, make him poison his own tail.

My mouth gapes to scoop the spider's brood, Leviathan straining krill, their dying embers tickling my throat.

My gulf-spanning shriek scares the crow back to the rim of time. My claws snap the hunter's arrow and my teeth drive him back into the day.

A single strike, the ring of the prince's arms severed at the wrists.

All of you

watch as it ends, as my own curtain descends, as I add your blue bauble to my hoard, warm you against my belly, my sleeping egg.

Epilogue: Lies

In the end they're all consumed,
just as you and I, in that world or our own
are fodder for the heartless sun
that crushes all with chariot wheels,
its dream-slaying curtain drug behind
to show us our true predators
are close at hand, close as our hands,
as the blocking we follow on this slum-rot stage
when our gazes cannot fix upon the stars—
we play our parts
and pray our strands of plot won't end
until the night begins again,
the tales resume.

The Monster in the Margins: An Afterword

Why on earth would anyone choose a career in poetry?

Science fiction poetry, yet?

As a co-worker and friend once put it to me. "That's obscure, man. That's really obscure." Context: as a music critic who covers a lot of underground and indie bands, he meant it as a compliment.

That's how I've come to think of myself, really, when it comes to these ditties—as The Misfits or Motörhead to someone else's Metallica.

I'm sure it sounds like a cliché to claim that I didn't choose poetry—poetry chose me. Yet in a significant way, it's simply the truth.

I'm chronically unable to focus on any one form of art, see—so I tried my hand at all of them. Some, like music, didn't stick past my teen years. Some, like writing novels, didn't stick at all until middle age, when the part of my brain that could manage long term tasks finally matured. Some, like poetry, especially poetry, glommed on early and grew, absorbing more and more of me, a symbiotic partner and parasite.

Editors bought my poems. I wrote more. The cycle repeated and repeated. I started pushing harder to learn the nuances of the craft, and to get my poetry in front of people. I won awards, spoke to college classrooms, got reviewed in a major newspaper, reprinted in "best of" volumes, recited in a little auditorium at the Library of Congress, had work translated, performed on stage before packed houses (though not packed because of my presence)—remained obscure. I'd be liar though if I claimed I didn't have fun.

These days, I don't write so much poetry. I jump between novel writing and anthology editing, with little room left in between.

Yet as you can see, if you made it this far in the book without skipping to the end, over twenty-some years, a few poems here and a few poems there can an accumulate into a mighty mass of words.

Which leads me to this special volume's humble origins. Honestly, I began 2013 with no plans whatsoever to release a new collection of poetry. They're awfully hard to sell, you see, even more so for someone obscure like me.

Thus the spark for this book was struck almost accidentally. Recently I ran a pair of successful Kickstarter campaigns—one for producing a new volume in my weird fiction anthology series, *Clockwork Phoenix*; the other for revitalizing my long running journal *Mythic Delirium*. Brainstorming rewards for the latter with my good friend and amazing supporter Elizabeth Campbell, I hit upon the idea of offering an omnibus poetry collection in ebook form. After all, I've had a smidgen of success in the newfangled world of Kindle, and none of my poetry collections were available in that format. Elizabeth gamely offered to help make the book.

Once the Kickstarter succeeded, and I'd committed to making this book, I realized that assembling an ebook omnibus would be a grossly impractical labor. I've written a lot of poems, after all. I asked Dominik Parisien if he'd be willing to act as editor for the book, and he agreed to the challenge.

I believe in serendipity, and some fortuitous events dovetailed that helped shape this collection. *Goblin Fruit* editor Amal El-Mohtar selected my multi-part poem "Hungry Constellations" for her publication's Fall 2013 feature. Of all the poems I've written over the past five years, that's the one I'm most proud to have set down in pixels. Not to mention, I've long hoped to have a *Goblin Fruit* feature of my very own. So once that happened, I knew it had to be in the book, and had to be the title piece.

It so happened, when Dominik read it, that he chose to make it the anchor of the collection, and that the poem's imagery inspired Paula Friedlander's amazing cover illustration.

The poems in this book appear in the order Dominik chose for them. His selections have taught me some interesting things about what inspires me to write poems—it's not been as solitary a practice as I've tricked myself into thinking. So often my poems are written as presents for people, or at their request, or sparked by anecdotes they've told or stories they've written. Some are responses to striking works of visual art. Some were first written to be performed on stage. Some serve as personal eulogies for the departed.

The connections evident to me in every page make me feel as if I'm flipping through a photo album, revisiting scenes from my creative life, and through their translucent surfaces, viewing other threads of time refracted and recombined.

For this I'm glad for *all* the time I've spent horseplaying in the margins.

About the Author

On weekdays, Mike Allen writes the arts column for the daily newspaper in Roanoke, Va. Most of the rest of his time he devotes to writing, editing, and publishing. His first novel, a dark fantasy called *The Black Fire Concerto*, appeared in 2013, and he's written a sequel, *The Ghoulmaker's Aria*, that's in the revision stage.

He raised more than $10,000 through a Kickstarter campaign to revive his anthology series dedicated to boundary-blurring work, *Clockwork Phoenix*. That Kickstarter funded *Clockwork Phoenix 4*, released in 2013 to much critical acclaim. He also edits and publishes *Mythic Delirium*, which began in 1998 as a poetry journal; a second Kickstarter campaign in 2013 rebooted it as a digital publication for poetry and fiction. In other words, 2013 was a big year for him, and 2014 isn't far behind, with the release of his sixth poetry collection, *Hungry Constellations*, and his first collection of short fiction, *Unseaming*. Somewhere in there he squeezes in time for an audio column, "Tour of the Abattoir," which appears in mostly monthly intervals at *Tales to Terrify*.

He receives a ton of help with all this editing from his wife, artist and horticulturalist Anita Allen. Their pets, Loki (canine) and Persephone and Pandora (feline) provide distractions. You can follow Mike's exploits as a writer at descentintolight.com, as an editor at mythicdelirium.com, and all at once on Twitter at @mythicdelirium.

ACKNOWLEDGMENTS

"Introduction" by Amal El-Mohtar. Copyright © 2014 by Amal El-Mohtar.

"The Strip Search" first performed for stage at Mill Mountain Theatre, Waldron Stage, Roanoke, Va., April 15, 2005. First print appearance in *Strange Horzions*, Oct. 3, 2005.

"The Strange Wisdom of the Dead," original title "His True Epitaph," first appeared in *Penny Dreadful* #6, Winter 1998.

"finale" first appeared in *Strange Wisdoms of the Dead,* Wildside Press, 2006.

"Death of the Father" first appeared in *Petting the Time Shark and Other Poems*, DNA Publications, 2003.

"The Terrible Beauty of a Severed Neck" first appeared in *Star*Line* 28.5, Sept./Oct. 2005.

"Jars" first appeared in *Curbside Review*, Aug. 2002.

"that strange man with the green petunias" first appeared in *Strange Wisdoms of the Dead,* Wildside Press, 2006.

"Space War" first appeared in *Strange Horizons*, June 14, 2004.

"Mother" first appeared in *Epitaph* #3, 1997.

"Bizarremost Bazaar" first appeared in *Weird Tales* #333, Sept./Oct. 2003.

"The Psychic Above Burritoville" first appeared in *Strange Wisdoms of the Dead,* Wildside Press, 2006, and in *Jabberwocky 2*, ed. Sean Wallace, Prime Books, 2006.

"The Eyewish Station" first appeared in *Not One of Us* #34, Sept. 2005.

"The Night Watchman Dreams His Rounds at the REM Sleep Factory" first appeared in *Dreams and Nightmares* #69, Dec. 2004.

"The Dream Eaters" first performed for stage at Mill Mountain Theatre, Waldron Stage, Roanoke, Va., March 11, 2005. First print appearance in *Strange Wisdoms of the Dead,* Wildside Press, 2006.

"Phase Shift" first appeared in *Tales of the Unanticipated* #17, Winter 1997.

"Defacing the Moon" first appeared in *Scavenger's Newsletter* #160, June 1997.

"Godspore" first appeared in *Strange Wisdoms of the Dead,* Wildside Press, 2006.

"Aranea" © 2005 by Mike Allen and Sonya Taaffe. First appeared in *Not One of Us* #34, Sept. 2005.

"desolvation" first appeared in *Star*Line* 28.4, July/Aug. 2005.

"Momentum" first appeared in *Tales of the Unanticipated* #16, Spring 1996.

"Pulse" first appeared in *Strange Horizons*, Sept. 22, 2003.

"Eating the Time Shark" first appeared in *Strange Wisdoms of the Dead,* Wildside Press, 2006.

"Tithonus on the Shore of Ocean" first appeared in *Change*, ed. John Benson, Not One of Us, 2006.

"Retracing the Moon" first appeared in *The Journey to Kailash*, Norilana Books, 2008.

"The Asteroid Painter" first appeared in *Dreams & Nightmares* #67, 2004.

"Sackful of Satellites" first appeared in *Lone Star Stories* 22, Aug. 2007.

"Charon Finds a Woman on the Gridshore" first appeared in *The Journey to Kailash*, Norilana Books, 2008.

"The Journey to Kailash" first appeared in *Strange Horizons*, Jan. 23, 2006.

"Midnight Rendevous, Boston" first appeared in *EOTU Ezine*, June 2003.

"Midnight Rendevous, Eden" first appeared in *The Journey to Kailash*, Norilana Books, 2008. A portion of this poem appeared as "The Visitor" in *Aoife's Kiss*, June 2004.

"Sisyphus Walks" first appeared in *Goblin Fruit*, Issue 1, Spring 2006.

"*lis pendens*" first appeared in *Strange Horizons*, June 26, 2006.

"Petals" first appeared in *Star*Line*, Vol. 31, Issue 2, 2008.

"The Captive Pleads With the Memory Carver" first appeared in *Tales of the Unanticipated* #26, 2005.

"Strange Cargo" first appeared in *Strange Horizons*, Dec. 6, 2004.

"Bacchanal" first appeared in *Goblin Fruit*, Issue 3, Autumn 2006.

"The Thirteenth Hell" first appeared in *The Journey to Kailash*, Norilana Books, 2008.

"The Disturbing Muses" first appeared in *Disturbing Muses*, Prime Books, 2005.

"O'Keeffe's Bones" first appeared in *Disturbing Muses*, Prime Books, 2005.

"Tanguy's Pebble" first appeared in *Disturbing Muses*, Prime Books 2005.

"Picasso's Rapture" first appeared in *Strange Horizons*, June 6, 2005.

"La Donna del Lago" first appeared in *Strange Horizons*, Aug. 22, 2011.

"Carrington's Ferry" first appeared in *Strange Horizons*, Jan. 23, 2012.

"Machine Guns Loaded with Pomegranate Seeds" first appeared in *Strange Horizons*, Nov. 19, 2012.

"Ascending" first appeared in *Strange Horizons*, Jan. 5, 2009.

"Sisyphus Crawls" first appeared in *Fantastique Unfettered #4*, Winter 2011/2012.

"The King of Cats, the Queen of Wolves" © 2011 by Mike Allen, Nicole Kornher-Stace and Sonya Taaffe. First appeared in *Apex Magazine* 22, March 2011.

"The Parcae" first appeared in *Jabberwocky 4*, Erzebet YellowBoy & Sean Wallace, eds., Prime Books, 2009.

"To Sail the Leaden Sky," first appearance here.

"The Problem with Science Fiction Poetry" first appeared in *Space and Time*, Summer/Fall 2008.

"Kandinsky's Galaxy" first appeared in *Strange Horizons*, April 9, 2012.

"Deluge" first appeared in *Strange Horizons*, Nov. 16, 2009.

"TimeFlood" © 2005 by Mike Allen and Ian Watson. First appeared in *Asimov's Science Fiction*, Feb. 2005.

"Seed the Earth, Burn the Sky" first appeared in *Fantastique Unfettered #4*, Winter 2011/2012.

"Surviving Wonderland" first appeared in *Stone Telling*, Issue 5, Oct. 2011.